"Gillian, I doubt you wanted to meet to discuss soda."

"No," She took a deep breath. "Your boss knows your abilities better than I do. If he doesn't want you on the case, then I don't want you trying to help on your own."

"I told you. I lost my head once. It won't happen again. Besides, how do you know what I'm doing?"

Gillian's eyes held a wealth of knowledge and what almost looked like pain. "I doubt you're trailing me for any other reason."

The past rose between them, an untreated wound.

Unwilling to hold her gaze, Brad stared past the bushes to the tall, study trees that provided relief from the sun. "You're right."

Gillian fiddled with her paper cup. "Then you need to back off."

"*You* know why I can't. For the record, I didn't lose it until after we nabbed the guy."

"Then why haven't you been assigned to the case?"

Brad stared again at the trees. "He doesn't know why I lost it."

Dear Reader,

Every book and every story is special to an author. The most special, though, are those that connect powerfully with you, the reader. And I can't think of any stories more powerful or precious than those that contain children, touching on their happiness, their safety and our love for them.

Nor can I think of anything more wrenching than a story about a child who simply vanishes. Gone so quickly that, at first, no one believes it's true.

Brad Mitchell, an officer with the Houston Police Department, and Gillian Kramer, an FBI agent, have seen enough to know just how real child abductions are. They are brought together by this tragic search, but it's not the first time they've met. A year before, their perfect marriage had fallen apart. Now they must put aside their differences and work together to find this little girl....

I invite you to share their search, to find out if in working together they can solve the problems they had before.

Sincerely,

Bonnie K. Winn

Vanished

Bonnie K. Winn

HARLEQUIN®

TORONTO • NEW YORK • LONDON
AMSTERDAM • PARIS • SYDNEY • HAMBURG
STOCKHOLM • ATHENS • TOKYO • MILAN • MADRID
PRAGUE • WARSAW • BUDAPEST • AUCKLAND

ISBN 0-373-71139-5

VANISHED

For my brave son, Brian, and his beautiful bride, Lindsey.
And to Laura Shin. Thank you.

PROLOGUE

GILLIAN STARED INTO her husband's eyes, eyes that could darken with passion…or anger. Now, however, they were clouded with confusion, regret. Feelings she shared.

Unable to resist the motion, she lifted her hand to tenderly stroke his cheek, feeling the faint tremor beneath clenched muscles. A question formed on Brad's face, but she slid her fingers down to gently still his lips.

They had been through all the questions hundreds of times. But there were no answers. Not for them. Gillian's glance fell on a framed picture of the two of them. They were both laughing. The photo had been taken shortly after they married, a magical time.

Then and later everyone thought she and Brad were the perfect couple—that their union would last forever. But no one else knew the truth…or the secrets. So, now they stood on the edge of goodbye.

"Gillian, it doesn't have to be this way," Brad urged.

There was no solution for the tear in their marriage, no possibility that it could ever be made right. But that didn't stop the aching. "There's no other way," she replied quietly, picking up her suitcase. "Not for us."

"You're being stubborn," he insisted.

Her smile was sad, tinged with regret and irony. She wasn't the only stubborn one. But this wasn't a matter of an inability to compromise. If it were only that easy.

Gently she put her lips against his one final time. Pulling back she searched the face that was so dear to her. The breaking of her heart was a near physical wound. Silently she uttered the words that had once held them so fast. *I will always love you, Brad Mitchell.*

Always.

CHAPTER ONE

One year later

THE NIGHT WAS DARK. Ideal for his purpose.

As was the house. It had taken time to select both the perfect child and setting. He issued a silent, contemptuous laugh. Few would appreciate the extensive work he poured into each endeavor, the careful planning, the flawless execution.

But the end result always held the public's attention.

The low bedroom window was easy to reach. Once inside, he spread a drop cloth to catch any stray hair or flake of skin. His clothing, hat, gloves and face mask covered his flesh, but he was taking no chances.

As he'd known it would be, the room was lit by a night-light, making it easy to navigate around the few scattered toys. Nine-year-old Katie Johnson slept the untroubled sleep of the young. But he was too smart, too experienced to waste precious time savoring the sight.

Chloroform to her mouth and nose rendered the child unconscious before she could utter even the tiniest squeal of protest. Leaving as he'd entered, he placed Katie's body in a second cloth before retrieving the one from her room.

Taking great care, he made sure the window and screen were left as he found them. The springy grass of the well-tended lawn assured him there would be no detectable footprints.

It would be hours before Katie's parents discovered she was gone. And by the time the police were contacted, he and his newest doll would have disappeared.

Back in his van, he allowed himself a superior smile at the ease of it all. The police never understood that *he* was the hunter. Dragnets could never compare with the sheer brilliance of his work.

The dark van blended with the moonless night. Driving cautiously, he garnered no attention. But then, few were awake at 2:00 a.m. in a middle-class community. When the baffled neighbors were questioned, he was confident no one would report his presence.

The police would sermonize and threaten. But as always, the abduction would remain an open, unsolved case. He'd yet to find a cop that was his match. In the safety of his van, he laughed with true mirth. It was too bad the police were so stupid. Going head-to-head with them was a contest he would enjoy.

He glanced back at young Katie. Fortunately, there was much to enjoy already.

IT WASN'T A PRETTY PLACE. A soulless conference room, one that resembled hundreds, if not more, in police stations across the country. Utilitarian by nature, now it filled with tension as papers hit the wide, scarred table, followed by the clank of seldom-washed coffee mugs.

Voices competed in the cramped, stuffy room, no one bothering to lower their volume for another's conversation. It was usually like this, Brad Mitchell acknowledged, yet his gut tightened, reminding him why he'd wanted this assignment, how it still burned that he'd been turned down flat.

A spattering of detectives, along with a larger group of uniformed officers, continued to filter in, chairs scraping back as everyone settled into place.

It was always tense when the FBI was called in. Local hackles rose at the presumptuous authority of the feds. Especially in this case, which had been committed right in the precinct's backyard.

The kidnapping of a young girl. A despicable crime, one that sent every officer into overdrive. And for Brad it was personal. His younger sister, Amanda, had disappeared sixteen years ago. They'd never found her body or any evidence of what had happened to her. As time passed, the cops assigned to the investigation had moved on. Neither he nor his parents ever could.

Last night, nine-year-old Katie Johnson had been taken from her bed. She was the second child to be abducted in two months, which was why the FBI had been called in.

Impatiently, Brad drummed his fingers on the table, waiting for the meeting to begin. True, he wasn't assigned to the case, but his captain, Lou Maroney, hadn't barred him from the general briefing.

Brad fidgeted, guessing the meeting might be a huge waste of time. Unless the feds had canvassed all of Houston's five hundred square miles, he doubted they had anything new to add to the investigation. Meanwhile, children remained at risk. Despite Maroney's unwavering command, Brad needed to be on the streets, needed...

The thought faded away. Captain Maroney stood at the head of the table. But it wasn't Lou at whom Brad stared.

It was the dark-haired woman at his side. A woman with huge brown eyes and a heart-shaped face. A face that still intruded on Brad's dreams. The face of his ex-wife.

Lou introduced Gillian to the group, explaining that Special Agent Kramer was to be the FBI's lead on the task force.

Kramer, Brad thought inanely. *So Gillian had taken back her maiden name.* There had been no contact since the divorce, no intentional or accidental encounters. In a city of four million it was remarkably easy to never again see the person who had once been the center of his life.

He studied her hungrily, looking for signs of change, not certain whether or not to be disappointed to find few.

She hadn't aged. Smooth skin glowed despite the glare of unforgiving fluorescent lights. Her classical features were, if possible, even more beautiful. Glancing around he saw there was a fair share of male admiration directed her way.

She might be FBI, but she was all woman.

He had never lost sight of that fact, from the first supercharged moment they'd met to the agonized last goodbye. It would be torture to remember the time sandwiched between the two, Brad realized. Because he had believed their union was destined for a lifetime.

Gillian, however, seemed remarkably detached as she acknowledged Lou's introduction. "I can't say I'm pleased to be here," she began. "After all, it's a crime we all detest that's brought me to your station.

However, I *am* pleased to be working alongside the city's finest. Together I know we'll accomplish what each of us wants—we are going to find this perpetrator and put him away before another child is taken from her family. Right?''

Gillian looked satisfied as she glanced around the room, seeing heads nodding in agreement. It was only when she met Brad's gaze that she faltered. Although the pause was only momentary, the connection seemed palpable, freezing out everything else.

Afterward, Maroney gave instructions and officers began filtering into the squad room. Brad and Gillian remained behind, their steps awkward, hesitant as they narrowed the space between them.

''Well...Agent *Kramer*. Didn't take you long to start using your maiden name.'' As soon as the words were spoken, Brad cursed his lack of control.

Her gaze was guarded. ''We both decided it was over, time to get on with our own lives.''

''So we did.'' He stared at Gillian, wondering what was really going on beneath her calm expression. "You look good."

The slight uncertainty in Gillian's eyes began to fade. "You, too." Then one side of her mouth lifted. "Do you suppose every divorced couple says that when…" Her words faltered.

"They meet for the first time after everything's final?" He completed the sentence for her. A shrug accompanied the words, covering his reaction. "Probably. Why didn't you tell me you were coming here today?"

"How was I supposed to know you work out of this station?"

How indeed? After the divorce Brad had requested a transfer that put him on the opposite side of the city. Unlike most major metropolitan centers, Houston's huge land mass was more like a collection of villages and small towns, each with its own personality. He'd needed to claim one for his own, one that he hadn't shared with Gillian.

Questions lurked in her eyes when he didn't immediately reply.

From experience he was able to shake

away the thoughts. They had no place here. "You're right—you couldn't have known. But this is my part of town now." He hadn't intended to sound territorial, but the words echoed with proprietorship.

Eyebrows, arched perfectly by nature rather than an esthetician, lifted ever so slightly. "Just like this is your sort of case?"

Brad clenched his jaw. It was difficult enough simply seeing Gillian again. But he hated to admit to her that he'd been shut out of this assignment. Instead he abruptly changed the subject. "Roger Turner's the HPD lead."

"I met him before the briefing. Along with Campbell, Spiers and Fulton." She gestured to a man lingering near the doorway. "My partner, Steve Savino."

The men sized each other up as she introduced them.

Gillian spoke to her partner. "I was about to tell Detective Mitchell that I'm ready to meet with the detectives on the task force."

Brad pointed out a cramped room down the hall. "Use my office. It's the second one on the left. I'll round up the troops."

As Brad walked away, Gillian stared after him wryly. Brad probably didn't even realize he'd taken her acquiescence for granted.

Glancing up, she saw that Savino lingered.

He didn't comment. "You still want me to set up the database on tips?"

"Yes. Let's proceed as we discussed this morning according to the CASMIRC plan." The Child Abduction and Serial Murder Investigative Resources Center was the operational entity of the FBI. Gillian had been assured by Maroney that his department was grateful for the federal resources the program supplied.

Savino headed for the computer station that had been designated for his use as Gillian headed toward Brad's office. Her pace slowed as a strong, unexpected curiosity seized her. She'd often wondered what Brad had been doing since they'd been apart.

His office didn't fill in the missing holes very well. There were stacks and stacks of papers, along with some Chinese take-out cartons, which appeared to have been ordered some time ago. But no family photos sat on the desk, and only framed degrees and commendations broke up the stark white walls. It was one of the contradictions that made Brad such an enigma. No outward sense of close family, yet he could never really forget what his family had gone through in the past.

Hearing footsteps, she turned quickly.

A red-haired woman was the first to enter the office. Her smile was nearly as vibrant as her hair.

"Detective Campbell," Gillian greeted her.

"Call me Vicki."

Shawn Spiers was directly behind her. His smile, too, was easy. Debra Fulton, a tall, striking blonde, sauntered in next.

Roger Turner pushed forward. "Why are we meeting in here? My office is across the hall."

"Chill," Debra told him lazily. "We're already here."

Before Gillian could question why Brad wasn't with the group, Turner took the floor. "We all know the urgency in catching this perp before another child is snatched." His eyes went from the detectives to Gillian. "And for that reason, there will be no politics. No tug-of-war over turf."

Debra Fulton studied her manicured nails. "You're the department lead, Roger. You haven't been promoted to captain just yet."

"And we know how to play nice with the FBI," Shawn added.

Turner sighed. "Agent Kramer—"

Despite the man's pompous attitude, she didn't plan to sit meekly by and allow Turner to take charge. It had already been agreed by the top brass, local and federal, that the FBI would be in charge of the investigation. Gillian was both the lead and liaison with the HPD. And Roger Turner would have to accept that. Just as Brad would, she realized, wondering again where he'd disappeared to. "Detective Turner, between your department's legwork and the federal resources we should be able to find a swift solution."

Roger Turner didn't look particularly pleased to be lumped in with his fellow detectives.

"You've all met my partner, Steve Savino. His primary function during this investigation will be to assess the tips received from the Amber Alert and assign officers to them.'' Gillian glanced around the room, seeing the team nod in agreement.

"As you know, Katie Johnson's photo and description have been distributed.'' Gillian, like the other officers and agents, was grateful that the Amber Alert program had been developed. The system coordinated the efforts of law enforcement, the media and the public to recover abducted children. "Unfortunately we have no description of the suspect or vehicle to give out. And that will impede the public's ability to help us.''

The detectives' expressions were all grim.

"That doesn't mean I don't think we can find this child alive. Nor have I given up on Tamara Holland.'' She paused, giving them a moment to reflect on ten-year-old Tamara, the first girl who'd been abducted eight weeks earlier. "We now have all resources at our disposal, federal labs and databases.''

"Detectives Spiers and Campbell, you were first respondents on Tamara Holland?''

"After the uniforms,'' Spiers replied.

"MO was the same. Entrance through ground-floor bedroom window. No note demanding ransom. Trace evidence, unfortunately, nonexistent."

"Follow-up on the parents?" Gillian questioned.

"Yes," Vicki replied. "Initially we questioned their stories because they didn't quite add up. Then we learned that Mr. Holland was with another woman at the time he reported being at work. It checked out. The hotel clerk confirmed his statement. Holland didn't want his wife to find out about the affair on the same day their daughter disappeared."

Gillian nodded. "Agent Savino will be reviewing interviews with all witnesses on both victims." She glanced around. "Does anyone have the duty roster Captain Maroney drew up?"

Turner shifted through the papers he held, handing her a single sheet. She scanned it, not seeing Brad's name. Hiding her surprise, she glanced back at him. "I don't see Detective Mitchell listed on the roster."

"He's not assigned to this case," Turner told her with satisfaction.

She concealed her reaction. "Since he sat in on the briefing, I assumed he was part of the team."

"Captain gave Brad the usual hands-off." Debra Fulton responded before Turner could.

"Gory details aren't necessary," Spiers added, still casual, but now more watchful. "He's got a conflict of interest. Something personal but nothing you'll have to worry about."

Gillian swallowed past the sudden lump in her throat, the memories nearly flattening her. That little bit of nothing had taken away everything she'd valued.

She reached for her most professional tone. "This crime gets to everyone." As she pushed forward with the meeting, a singular thought lingered. What had happened to Brad in the past year? What had he done to get himself banned from the very cases he'd gone into law enforcement to solve and prevent? And how in the world was she going to get over the emotions he still stirred?

CHAPTER TWO

LATE THAT AFTERNOON Brad had no trouble tailing Gillian's black Eclipse. But short of bugging her car, he didn't know what she was learning. He'd extended his lunch hour to follow her, yet Brad knew this method wasn't going to get him any nearer to the actual case. And he couldn't ask Shawn Spiers to keep him informed. It was one thing to go out on his own limb, another to drag a friend along.

The stoplight changed from yellow to red as Gillian glided through the intersection. Not concerned, Brad waited out the red, confident he could easily pick up her trail again. But by the time he reached the next intersection, he still hadn't found her.

Before the light could change, Brad felt a mild impact as his car was nudged from behind. Swearing beneath his breath, Brad hoped the other driver would agree to drive away. He started to glance in the rearview mirror, but his cell phone rang and he answered it. Police business came before minor fender benders.

Maroney's impatient voice came through the slim phone.

Brad glanced at his watch, realizing he'd been gone longer than he'd intended. As he considered his explanation, he saw a shadow fall across him, then a body blocked the light coming in his open driver's side window. And despite his captain's steady dialogue, all Brad could do was stare.

Gillian bent over, planting her hands on the window opening as she leaned closer. "You looking for me?"

Since she'd spoken loud enough for Lou Maroney to hear, the captain started sputtering and Brad could almost see his long, thin face flushing the way it did when he was really ticked.

Completing his phone call by agreeing to head back to the station to meet with his boss immediately, Brad pushed open his door as Gillian stepped back.

"Cute," he commented, angling his head toward her car. He'd seen easily that she'd bumped his SUV with such precision that neither car had sustained any damage.

"I wasn't trying to be," she replied, crossing her arms.

"Then what gives?"

"Shouldn't I be asking that?" she demanded.

So she was angry. He should have guessed she would be. He should also have remembered how good she was at her job. Although his tailing had been expert, her detection was also.

"You're not assigned to the case, Brad. And I'm guessing from the squawks I just heard, that Maroney didn't know you were joining the hunt on your own."

Brad had little defense. Still he stepped a foot closer. "You know what this means to me."

Memories rushed between them, flattening, gut-wrenching memories.

Gillian looked at her trim loafers, the air of her anger dissipating, gradually deflating her stance. "Yeah. I know." She glanced back up at him. "But getting in my way isn't going to change the past and it sure won't help the children we have to save *now*."

Brad felt the increased presence of the desperation that never completely left him. "You don't know that. With my experience—"

"You could be a liability," Gillian said bluntly. "I'm not trying to be unkind, but I have to be honest. Your experience *should* be a help, but obviously it hasn't been or Maroney wouldn't keep you off the case."

"I lost my head once," he admitted.

She met his gaze, her luminous dark eyes deepening with too much knowledge. Knowledge of him. "And we need calm, cool heads. You're not the victim here, Brad, or even part of the victim's family. Their interests have to be first priority."

"I wouldn't have it any other way," Brad insisted. "That's why I want to help."

Gillian glanced down and then away. "I know. Look, I don't have time for this discussion right now. And from the sound of your telephone conversation, you don't, either."

Not waiting for his response, she walked to her car and slid inside. Within moments she was speeding past him. He pounded the hood of his vehicle, but the motion didn't begin to vent his repressed emotions.

And only the impatient honking of waiting cars made him climb into his SUV to make his way back to the station.

IT DIDN'T TAKE LONG for Brad to reach the precinct house, but he found his steps lagging before he got to Captain Maroney's office. The two of them went back a long way. Lou had been Brad's first commander when he was a raw rookie straight from the academy.

It hadn't been an accident when Brad had applied for a transfer to this particular precinct. Houston was large enough that he could have picked a dozen others. But Lou Maroney was a good man, one who hadn't asked about Brad's reasons for moving. However, he had zeroed in quickly on Brad's vulnerability on cases involving missing children. Luckily, not that many had fallen under their jurisdiction. But after working one, Brad hadn't been assigned any others.

Stepping into his commander's office, Brad anticipated the contents of the coming lecture. The red flush Brad had expected on Maroney's face had faded.

"Shut the door," Maroney greeted him.

So it was going to be a real yellfest, Brad thought, shutting the door, then dropping into a chair. "Ran into some traffic getting back to the station."

Maroney stared at him steadily. "Is that what tied up your entire morning as well?"

"I was—"

"Don't bother. We both know what you were doing. Can't say it came as a surprise. Didn't actually expect the FBI to be within hearing distance, though."

"I didn't, either."

"No problem. You're to stay *out* of this case. Completely."

"Lou, I went over my lunch hour about twenty minutes. It's not as though I ever cut my time short. But if it'll make you feel better, I'll skip lunch tomorrow."

"No," Maroney replied. "It won't."

Brad frowned. "What's wrong?"

"You're usually sharper on the uptake. Brad, you aren't to approach the detectives or agents assigned to this case to so much as ask if they want coffee. You do and you're on suspension."

"Suspension?"

Maroney's face was sober, unrelenting. "Until the case is resolved. Do we understand each other?"

"You don't mean that."

"I've never meant anything more. I intend to make sure Katie Johnson returns home safely. And, God willing, Tamara Holland. I can't take the chance you'll screw that up."

"I lost my head *once,* but only *after* we caught the perp. It didn't compromise the case."

"That's because the victim was already dead." Maroney's voice held no inflection. "If you were to lose your head while the victims are still alive—"

"That's not going to happen."

"I'm not taking any chances."

Brad could scarcely believe Lou would

take this unreasonable stance. "And you'd suspend me rather than take advantage of my experience?"

"While you're working for me, you're staying out of the investigation."

Brad met his boss's gaze and saw no leeway there. "Fine."

"Just like that?" Maroney's eyes narrowed in suspicion.

"Pretty much. Effective tomorrow, I'm taking a leave of absence and I won't be working for you."

Now Maroney's thin cheeks did flush red with anger. "Damn it, Mitchell! You can't be of any help on this case."

"That's where you're wrong, Lou. I'll fill out my paperwork and have it on your desk this afternoon. I have years of vacation and sick days built up."

"Brad, I can't stop you from requesting leave, but for God's sake, think about what you're doing!"

Brad met Maroney's eyes. "That's exactly what I *am* doing."

"If you get in the way, it'll cost you your badge," Maroney warned.

No one understood, Brad realized. But that wasn't going to deter him. No one could. Not Maroney, not even his ex-wife.

THAT EVENING GILLIAN entered her apartment wearily. She'd spent the day in the field interviewing Katie Johnson's parents and much of her family, then meeting individually with the detectives on the task force, and it was well after eleven o'clock before she headed home.

Kicking off her loafers, Gillian dropped her purse on the hall table, keeping the stack of file folders in her hands. She needed to read all of them before morning.

Feet sinking into the deep pile of the pale peach carpet, she padded through the semilit living room. She had deliberately chosen the feminine furnishings, hoping to wipe out thoughts of Brad and the home they'd shared. Somehow, it just emphasized her loneliness that much more.

The decor was not what she would have chosen when she was married. Plumping a pillow, she ran her fingers over the textured fabric. No, then she'd thought in terms of how to make their home one a man could ease into like a favorite pair of jeans. Now it looked more like a delicate evening gown. One for a very single woman.

The phone rang, interrupting the first quiet of her day. Gillian considered ignoring it, but the ties of both family and job had her picking it up on the second ring.

Her sister, Teri, didn't bother with routine greetings. Instead she launched into a diatribe on what was wrong with each member of the PTA, from a parent's perspective. Although Teri had once been a special-education teacher herself, she'd stayed home after the birth of her twins.

"Too bad you can't work up a real opinion," Gillian replied wryly when Teri paused to take a breath.

Teri snickered. "Sorry. David's out of town and I haven't talked to anyone over five today."

Knowing her sister's hands were full caring for the children without David's help at bath and bedtime, Gillian found that special place in her heart for family warming. "Teri, what in the world are you doing phoning me? And don't give me that 'I need to talk to an adult' baloney.''

"Well, I *do* enjoy speaking with someone who's graduated from junior high school, at least," Teri defended weakly. "Okay, fine. Just wanted to make sure you're doing okay."

Although Gillian had been working long hours for several years, her parents and siblings still worried when she didn't answer her phone at ten in the evening. She hesitated, wondering how much she should share with her sister. "I'm okay."

"That was said with a notable lack of conviction."

The silence hummed between them for a few seconds.

"All right, Gillian, give. What's the matter?" Gillian could almost feel her sister's concern across the phone lines.

Teri's familiar comforting tones got to her. "I had somewhat of a shock today."

"Shock?"

Hearing similar shock in Teri's voice, Gillian sighed. "Nothing horrific." She closed her eyes, trying to keep the quiver from her voice. "I saw Brad today."

"Oh, Gilly!"

The tears Gillian had been holding back escaped. "It really shook me."

"Of course it did. Do you want me to come over? Damn! David's out of town. Do you want to come here?"

Gillian shook her head.

"I'm guessing you're shaking your head no," Teri said after a brief pause.

Sniffling, Gillian grasped the phone closer. "I'm exhausted, Teri. I had to act like seeing my ex-husband was just a run-of-the-mill experience."

Teri clucked sympathetically.

"And I'm working with locals I just met today—going in as the lead."

"There probably wasn't a moment alone to sort out your feelings about seeing Brad."

Gillian didn't speak for a moment, staring out of her window at the dark night. "My past didn't so much creep up on me, instead it slammed right into the present."

"I know it hurts," Teri replied gently.

"Like hell," Gillian admitted. "I knew I'd see him eventually, but…"

"It wouldn't have been easy regardless of the circumstances, sweetie."

"He asked why I didn't tell him I was going to be at his precinct. As though I knew."

"That was diplomatic of him."

Gillian picked up on the mild sarcasm. "What?"

"You know I liked Brad—a lot. But I didn't like the way he hurt you."

"The divorce was *my* idea," Gillian reminded her.

"That's semantics and you know it. He walked away unscathed and you, you…"

Gillian flinched and Teri seemed to sense it over the phone.

"I'm sorry, Gillian. That's the problem of speaking only with kids. You forget to think before you blurt out the first thing that springs to mind."

"It's okay. This topic's always a minefield, well-thought-out or not." Gillian wondered yet again if that would ever fade, if her marriage would become simply a barely remembered event from her past.

"Yeah," Teri agreed, with the truth only a sister only speak. "Still, I want to offer support, not more grief."

"Hey, I know you're always there for me."

"You sure you don't want to come over?"

"I have a real early morning tomorrow. This case is a killer and I'll need my wits about me."

"Okay, but I'm here if you need me."

With the connection broken, Gillian slowly replaced the receiver, surrounded by silence. And the emptiness in her apartment seemed even more lamentable.

CHAPTER THREE

BRAD HAD NEVER CONSIDERED how it would feel to be working on a case without the ability to flash his badge when needed. Or how he'd feel having to ask his ex-wife about the case.

He wasn't being especially careful or vigilant about following Gillian now. He'd lost her at a red light but knew she was heading back to the station. She was bound to realize he was tailing her before the morning was over—yesterday was proof of that.

His cell phone rang. He considered letting it go unanswered. There would be no urgent police work calling him.

Briefly cursing old habits, he snapped open the phone.

"Mitchell."

"Hello, *Mitchell,*" Gillian responded calmly.

He scanned the immediate area, wondering if she'd caught on to him already.

"Hello."

"I talked to Maroney this morning."

"Uh-huh."

"He told me about your leave of absence."

Brad glanced around again, but she wasn't behind him. "Yeah."

"So I'm wondering how long you plan to tail me."

Damn. She was even better than he'd given her credit for.

Gillian's voice broke the sudden silence. "I think we need to talk about this."

"I'm on my own time. Nothing that concerns you."

"Do you think your captain would agree?"

She had him there. "How about an early lunch?"

"I'm at the park about two blocks north," she replied. "There's a hot-dog vendor on the corner."

Brad remembered the days when all they'd needed were sloppy hot dogs in the park, laughter and love to be happy. Apparently she'd forgotten those times. Or they didn't carry the same memories for her. He sighed. It was, after all, just a hot dog. "Sure."

It took only a few minutes to reach the park and spot her Eclipse. Gillian was leaning back against the car. He knew she wasn't trying to be provocative, but that didn't matter. Trying to ignore his physical response, he parked quickly and got out.

Gillian met him halfway between their cars. "I only have a few minutes."

"Just enough time for a hot dog."

At the cart, Brad pulled out his wallet, while placing the order. "Two hot dogs, both with mustard and chili, one with kraut. A Coke and an orange soda."

As the man prepared their hot dogs, Gillian looked at Brad.

"What?" he asked.

"Just surprised you remembered my order."

For some strange reason, it bothered him that she thought he could so easily forget.

He shrugged in reply as they accepted the food and then strolled to an empty bench.

Brad unwrapped his steaming hot dog and tried to guess how long it would take Gillian to say what was on her mind.

As he wondered, she stared out across the park. A young mother with a toddler in one hand and an infant in a stroller paused by a small slide. The girl climbed the ladder, then shrieked in delight as she slid down into her mother's waiting arms.

Gillian pulled her gaze away, then took a small bite, washing it down with soda. "Not that many people drink orange soda anymore. It was lucky the vendor had some."

"I doubt you wanted to meet to discuss orange soda."

"No." She took a deep breath. "I have to believe that Maroney knows your abilities far better than I possibly could. If he doesn't want you on the case, then I don't want you trying to help on your own."

"I told you. I lost my head once. It won't happen again. Besides, how do you know what I'm doing?"

Gillian's eyes held a wealth of knowledge

and what almost looked like pain. "I doubt you're trailing me for any other reason."

The past rose between them, an untreated wound.

Unwilling to hold her gaze, Brad stared out at the green bushes, past to the tall, sturdy trees that provided relief from the overheated sun. "It's about the kidnapping."

A beat of silence echoed after the roar of a passing truck faded.

Gillian fiddled with her paper cup. "Then you need to back off."

"*You* know why I can't. And I won't be a liability. For the record, I didn't lose it until after we nabbed the guy."

"Then why hasn't Maroney assigned you to the case?"

Brad stared again at the dense greenery. "He doesn't know why I lost it."

Puzzlement filled Gillian's eyes. "Why didn't you tell him?"

Brad swallowed, remembering. "I considered it. But it's not as though we get this kind of case often."

"Yet you still didn't tell Maroney."

"Gillian, I don't know how it works with the feds, but in the HPD, telling your superior that you have an emotional connection to a certain type of crime isn't considered an asset."

She nodded. "I suppose so. But you could explain—"

"How long ago it was?" Brad asked bitterly. To him it seemed like yesterday. Part of him wanted to push away the memories, to keep the horror at bay. But a stronger need to make sure what happened to Amanda—and his family—didn't happen again tore at him as it had since he was fourteen years old. Closing his eyes, Brad remembered.

It had been like any other day. He'd had football practice after school. When he arrived home, even though Amanda wasn't there, he hadn't been concerned. He'd thought she was at Stacy's. The two girls had alternated between each other's houses nearly every day after school. He hadn't known Stacy wasn't in school that day because she was ill. It was only when his mother arrived home from work that they'd questioned Amanda's whereabouts. By then, his sister and her abductor had vanished.

In his mind, Amanda remained an enchanting twelve-year-old eager to be a teenager, yet who still slept in a bed filled with stuffed toys. Brad was always the big brother, and it had been his responsibility to watch out for her. Even today, he thought of himself as a failure.

He felt a gentle touch on his arm, a remembered touch. "Are you okay, Brad?"

Nodding, he put the past away for the moment. "Yeah."

"*This* is why you shouldn't be involved in the investigation," she said quietly, with no anger or censure. "You can't possibly remain objective."

"That's a pretty hasty assumption."

"No one could expect you not to feel a personal connection. Don't you see that?" she questioned, her hand still on his arm.

The point of connection seemed to grow warmer. He looked down, which must have made her follow his gaze.

Abruptly she pulled back. "I know this must be hard for you—to stand back and watch, but you have to put these new victims first.''

''Can you name anyone else in the department who's had as much training and experience?''

Her chin lifted a notch. ''And if I could?''

''You'd shut me out to even old scores?'' he asked incredulously.

Now her neck was stiff, her eyes level with his. ''I wasn't aware of any old scores.''

No, their marriage had been dissolved with near surgical precision.

He was the first to drop his eyes. ''You're right. I just—''

''Lost sight of the moment?'' she asked with jarring accuracy.

''I think I'm allowed this one. I'm not sure there's an established precedent on how to react when talking to your ex for the first time since the divorce. I don't recall a course on it at the academy.''

She pushed back a lock of hair that brushed her forehead. He'd always liked the relaxed, easy swing of her hair, the way the sunlight brought out the glossy dark sheen.

He had to consciously keep his hand from reaching out to touch the strands.

Luckily Gillian didn't notice his interrupted gesture. She crumpled her napkin and shoved it onto the paper tray that held the remainder of her uneaten hot dog. "Okay. We can agree on that."

"So what's your answer?"

To her credit she didn't pretend that she didn't know the bottom line. "I'll have to think about it."

"And meanwhile—"

"Meanwhile everything is being handled."

He wanted more, but he could see from her expression that was all he was going to get. And that had never been enough.

THREE HOURS LATER, and Gillian was stalled. She'd conducted interviews since early that morning and now she was waiting for Turner and Fulton to call. Afraid that her mind was becoming too cluttered with personal concerns, she'd decided to get away for an hour.

Gillian drove past the borders of the precinct toward her sister's home. When she'd phoned, Teri hadn't sounded quite so wound up now that David was back in town.

Gillian pulled into the driveway, appreciating as she always did the house's distinctive contemporary style. Hard and sleek lines camouflaged the warmth within.

Seemingly mile-high walls were primarily glass; window upon window that allowed the sunlight to cascade over the cool terrazzo and oak-planked floors. Teri insisted the design was easy to maintain. But it was clear the layout had been planned down to the last detail. Guests always lingered at Teri and David's parties, drawn into the charm of the house as well as the charisma of its owners.

From habit, Gillian opened the gate to the breezeway that led to both the terrace and the rear door.

"I'm back here," Teri called. She was sprawled on one of the swings that were cozily made for two people, her sandaled feet hanging over one side.

"All alone?" Gillian asked in surprise, seeing no kids running like mad in the thick grass. She wanted to talk to Teri alone and had been prepared to bribe her with an invitation to her favorite coffeehouse.

"Yep," Teri answered with obvious satisfaction. "David's taking the kids out to a movie as a treat."

"He is?" Gillian questioned with a trace of suspicion. Her sister and brother-in-law still acted like newlyweds. Gillian would have expected them to be together on his first day back.

"Just enjoy the blessed quiet. Oh, and there's peach iced tea on the table."

"Teri!" Gillian said with exasperation. "What are you doing getting rid of your wonderful husband on his first day home?"

Teri shrugged, the gesture of a woman confident of her marriage. "You wanted an audience?"

"Well, no, but I only planned to steal you away for an hour."

"David just moved up his day out with the kids. It's okay." Teri straightened a fraction, leaning toward her sister. "And you needn't worry I'm taking him for granted. Anything but. I know how lucky I am." She

met Gillian's eyes. "How very, very lucky
I am."

Gillian tried to halt the rush of emotions
that threatened to overwhelm her. There was
nothing like a sister, and none other in the
world like hers. Teri had kept her from completely falling apart after the divorce. She
had devoted hours to listening. And apart
from being protective, for the most part she
hadn't judged. Of course, she had bristled
over the fact that her little sister had been
hurt. But that came with the concern.

Reaching for a glass of iced tea, Gillian
fiddled with the pitcher for a moment, a de-
laying tactic she should have known her sister would recognize.

"Come, sit down," Teri said in a gentle
tone.

Gillian did as she asked, perching in a
solo rocker near her sister, then releasing a
huge sigh.

"That bad?" Teri asked.

"It's just…just…" Gillian stared out into
the pretty, well-tended yard. "Confusing,
strange…I don't know."

"That's understandable. Couldn't you ask

for a reassignment? I mean, if your boss understood your history with Brad—''

''You remember how glad I was to get my promotion so I could move on to a new office—with new people. It's hard to be around people who know all the gruesome details of your history. Sympathetic looks from the women. And from the men, being asked on dates either out of pity or on the assumption I'd be easy pickings. So, I really don't want to confide in my new boss.''

Teri nodded, then drank slowly from her tall glass. ''Funny, isn't it? I mean that both you and Brad are in different places with your work.''

''Well, that happens,'' Gillian mused. ''And I couldn't control my promotion.''

''Maybe.''

Gillian stared at her sister. ''Maybe?''

''What did you think would happen when you worked all those extra hours, weekends and holidays?''

''You make it sound like some sort of nefarious plot!''

''Calm down, baby sister. I doubt it was a conscious decision. But deep inside, maybe you hoped a career change would help you get over the loss of your marriage.''

"I don't know." Gillian shrugged. "I suppose so. But unlike Brad, I didn't ask for a transfer that would take me across town!"

"Ouch," Teri replied mildly.

Mentally, Gillian backpedaled. "I didn't mean it that way."

"If you didn't, you wouldn't be human." Teri reached out, patting her sister's arm. "Could you ask for a reassignment without revealing any personal reasons? Maybe tell your boss that you have a personal emergency, need to take some time off. Then, wouldn't they assign someone else to this case?"

"Wouldn't that be ironic," Gillian muttered.

"Ironic? Why?"

"Because Brad just took a leave of absence so he *could* work on the case."

Puzzled, Teri stared at her. "Why'd he have to do that?"

"His captain learned early on that Brad

can't keep his objectivity when it comes to child kidnappings.''

''Oh.'' Teri spoke the single word, but it resonated.

''Yeah. It's still tearing him up.''

''What about his family?'' Teri asked sympathetically.

''We aren't chummy enough to have discussed his parents.''

Teri caught Gillian's hand. ''Sweetie, this is going to rip you to pieces. Won't you consider talking to your boss?''

''I can't.'' Gillian bit her lip. ''I just *can't.*''

''But why not?''

''Because Amanda's disappearance eats at me, too,'' Gillian confessed, swiping at her eyes.

''It's who you are,'' Teri replied, reading her sister's thoughts. ''And because you loved Brad, it means nearly as much to you as it does to him.''

Gillian swallowed. ''And it was a big reason our marriage ended, not the whole of it, of course, but still…'' She left unsaid that it was a huge part of why her perfect love had shattered. Refusing to take the risk of being hurt by the disappearance of another child, Brad wouldn't even consider a baby. And Gillian couldn't consider a future without children. It was a stalemate that could never be resolved.

"So, now you have to figure out how to deal with Brad *and* this case," Teri said, her voice conveying her empathy.

"I know it won't be easy...."

"Sweetie, I just hope you live through it."

"Do you think I'm crazy?" Gillian asked solemnly.

"No. I think you're *you.* My very special sister who can't turn her back on a stolen child today or one from years ago. I just hate to think of the pain you're going to face."

Gillian couldn't force herself to deny that truth.

They sat together in easy silence. Years of caring and bonding eliminated the need to speak.

And in the quiet, Gillian remembered.

It had rained all day and much of the evening, leaving the black-topped road slick and the always humid air of Houston heavy with the remains of the storm. It was a dark night, the moon hiding beneath dense layers of clouds.

Brad had been assigned to an armed-robbery case, one that had begun locally, then crossed state lines. At that point the FBI had been called in to join the investigation.

Gillian had been part of the federal team. She and Brad had met inside a taped-off crime scene. Despite the murky night, their eyes had connected. The attraction had been instantaneous and enthralling.

The investigation ended quickly afterward, but not their romance. They fell in love, hard and fast. And with uncharacteristic abandon for both of them, they eloped within weeks of meeting. Despite the rush, their love was true and should have lasted forever.

Forever. The word reverberated through Gillian's thoughts. She still had days in which she woke expecting to find Brad beside her. And other, worse days, when she knew that would never happen again.

There had to be a reason why they'd been

thrown together again. She had a brief flash of his face, the sadness that still filled his eyes.

The scars were deep, unlikely to heal, but she had to try to help Brad. Even though they didn't have a future together, Gillian wanted him to be happy. And until he learned the value of family, Brad would never know that happiness.

Thinking of the missing children she had to find, Gillian prayed she was about to do the right thing. Gillian hugged her sister, then jogged to her car. Even the short hour she'd stolen was one she didn't have to spare.

As Gillian approached the precinct, she saw Brad sitting in his parked car. He casually waved and she couldn't repress an ironic smile as she motioned for him to follow.

Having come to what she hoped wasn't a disastrous decision, Gillian pulled into the lot of a small grocery store and parked, reaching into her portfolio for the latest case notes.

Brad knocked on her window.

Obligingly, Gillian rolled it down.

"You wanted to see me?"

"Uh-huh."

He let a few moments pass, glancing around the quiet lot. "You really shouldn't do surveillance alone. Is your partner still fielding leads from the public?"

"Uh-huh."

"Are you *trying* to be irritating?"

Gillian smiled sweetly. "No, it comes naturally."

He opened his mouth, then closed it as quickly.

She stuffed most of the papers back into her satchel. "As I see it, we have two alternatives. I can allow you to help or..."

Brad's eyes darkened.

"Or," she repeated. "I can send a report about you to both Captain Maroney and the head of the bureau." She paused. "So you have a decision to make."

"I'm listening."

Gillian bit her lip. "Here's my proposal. I'll agree that you can help *unofficially* with the investigation if you agree to my conditions.''

"Such as?"

"Interacting with me and my family."

"Your *family?*"

She lifted her brows at his tone. But it was up to Brad. He could choose to walk away. Although it hurt to admit it, he might prefer to give up this investigation rather than spend time with her.

Brad stepped a few inches closer. "Why this condition?"

Gillian knew her request must seem unusual to him. Brad hadn't interacted much with the Kramers during their brief marriage. She regretted not forcing the issue then. Perhaps if he had, he would have learned that family could bring fulfillment rather than loss. But she didn't think he was ready to hear that now. "Call me stubborn."

"I have. Often."

Gillian gripped her portfolio tightly, trying not to let emotion bleed into her voice. "So, what's it going to be?"

For several moments only the sounds of

passing traffic and the distant clatter from the store could be heard.

"I want to work this case," he said finally.

Gillian tried not to let his reluctance penetrate her professional stance. Or to stab at her frayed feelings. "Fine."

"Where to?"

"Brad, we need to get some ground rules established." She hadn't forgotten how he listened, then went his own way. This ability to remember every little detail about him, Gillian realized, could be a problem. She needed to keep her distance. "I don't want you to assume you're just one of the team. I shouldn't be including you in the investigation. Forget that I'm probably committing professional suicide. If I've made the wrong call, we aren't the ones who'll suffer." She reached to turn the key. "Are you getting in?"

Brad walked around the car and opened the passenger-side door. "You really should keep these locked."

History floated between them. "I can take care of myself."

His jaw tightened visibly. "So you can."

Gillian flipped on the defroster in defense against the muggy day. And wondered how she was going to keep the past where it belonged.

THE STREETS OF SOUTHWESTERN Houston were now as familiar to Brad as his own apartment. But he hadn't traveled them with Gillian at his side. She seemed detached, as though they'd never shared anything more intimate than work.

Gillian coasted to a stop at a red light. "I don't know much about this part of town."

"It's not really your style."

She looked at him. "And it's yours?"

He shrugged. "It suits me."

"I see." She turned on the next street, the one leading to Katie Johnson's elementary school.

It was one of the places young Katie had been the day she vanished. After school she had attended a Scout meeting nearby. FBI and HPD had canvassed the area continually since her disappearance.

Brad stared at the innocent-looking

school. "Who's investigating Deerling, the Scout leader?"

Gillian pulled alongside the curb, allowing traffic to pass. "That would be me. I interviewed him yesterday briefly, but I want to talk to him again."

All of Brad's instincts kicked in. "Cracking witnesses is my strong suit."

He hated that she stared at him as though she were evaluating a new acquaintance.

"This will be your test run." Gillian passed him a piece of paper she'd pulled from her notes earlier. "Here's the address of Mark Deerling's sister-in-law, Valerie Donnelly."

Brad held her gaze before dropping his eyes to scan the paper. "It's not far."

Gillian pushed at the hair that fell across her forehead. "Good."

Following his directions, Gillian took only a few minutes to reach the woman's house.

"She's his alibi?" Brad guessed.

"Or lack of it."

Valerie Donnelly opened her door, looking at them suspiciously. After introductions, she thawed. Patting her very pregnant abdomen, she led them into a toy-filled family room. "I'd apologize for the clutter. But I can't see the floor anymore. My husband's in charge of anything lying below eye level, but I've had him running around a lot lately."

"It's a very friendly room," Gillian replied.

"Has to be. We have three kids. And I'm expecting my fourth in a month." Valerie rolled her eyes. "Crazy thing is I'm excited about it."

Gillian cleared her throat. "We appreciate your time today."

"Of course. Not that I think I can tell you anything, but we've all been thinking about little Katie and her family nearly every moment since she disappeared. My brother-in-law, Mark—you've probably already talked to him—well, he's absolutely shattered."

"He was your sister's husband?"

Valerie nodded. "They were a true love match. Everyone thought they'd be together forever."

For a brief instant, instinct had Brad and Gillian looking at each other.

Gillian cleared her throat. "Your sister passed away?"

"Yes. Six years ago. A car accident. Thank God Mark wasn't hurt or the girls would be orphans." Valerie brushed at her eyes. "I'm sorry. It still hurts." She tried to laugh. "And I'm positively brimming with hormones." She reached for a tissue. "It was so hard for Mark. I thought we were going to bury him soon after."

"But..." Gillian prompted her.

"He had to go on for the girls. He's a remarkable man. He's taken on the whole load—work, the kids, PTA, even the Scouts." Valerie looked up at them. "Mark volunteered to take the girls' troop because Linda would have done it if she were alive. And he couldn't bear to know that the girls wouldn't have the experience because she wasn't there to keep it together."

"That kind of schedule must keep him busy," Brad observed.

"Yes. This may sound corny, but I think it actually helps him. Most men would have remarried by now, but Mark's devoted to Linda's memory."

Again Brad and Gillian's gazes met.

"I'm not sure what I can tell you about Katie Johnson," Valerie continued. "I wasn't able to participate in the searches Mark headed up."

Brad studied the woman. "I thought the neighborhood watch organized the searches."

Valerie nodded. "Yes. But Mark coordinated them. As soon as he heard about Katie, he volunteered."

"That was quite an undertaking," Gillian remarked.

"Yes," Valerie agreed. "But that's the kind of guy Mark is. Besides, he was so torn up, imagining if it had been one of his girls. They're everything to him."

"Understandable," Brad replied.

"To your knowledge did any strangers volunteer to help with the search?" Gillian asked.

Valerie shook her head. "No."

Brad watched her eyes, but saw nothing to indicate she was lying or hiding something. "Couldn't a stranger go unnoticed?"

"It's unusual these days, but we really

know our neighbors. This is an older area, some homeowners are second generation. So a stranger really sticks out.''

''Yet no one noticed anyone the night Katie disappeared.''

Valerie nodded sadly. ''And we've all questioned ourselves a million times about that.''

''Did you happen to see the troop that last meeting?'' Gillian questioned casually.

''No. I'm sorry. I wish I knew something, *anything* that would help.''

Gillian glanced at her notepad. ''One last thing, Mrs. Donnelly. Was Mark here Tuesday night?''

''Yes. His girls were having a sleepover with mine, so after the troop meeting Mark came over for dinner and videos.''

Videos that surely wouldn't have lasted into the wee hours.

Brad reached for his sunglasses. ''Do you know what time he left?''

Valerie scrunched her face in concentration. ''Must have been after eleven. I'm wiped out by ten, so it was a late night for me.''

Brad and Gillian stood in unison. "You've been a great help, Mrs. Donnelly."

Valerie started to rise.

"Please don't get up. We can see ourselves out," Gillian assured her.

Valerie looked greatly relieved. "If you're sure…"

"We are," Gillian replied.

Once outside, she and Brad headed toward the car.

"Gone by eleven, he had plenty of time to snatch Katie Johnson."

Brad nodded. "And if Deerling coordinated the volunteer searches, he could make sure any special hiding spot he set aside wouldn't be discovered."

"I'm not sure I buy the Saint Mark theory," Gillian agreed. "Scout leader, hasn't remarried, spends a lot of time with children who aren't his own. He was a little too quick with his answers yesterday. Everything seemed to fit *too* neatly."

Brad checked the second address Gillian had given him. "His house is only a few blocks away."

Deerling answered on the second ring and

opened the door widely to allow them to enter. Leading them into a tidy living room, he gestured to some comfortable-looking wing chairs.

"Please, sit down. Would you like coffee?"

Gillian and Brad shook their heads in unison.

Brad noticed and stopped the motion. "Not for me, thanks."

Deerling sat in a chair angled across from them. "Have you learned anything about Katie?"

"No," Gillian answered. "Not yet."

Brad studied the man as disappointment flashed across his face. Deerling was in the ideal position to have access to the girls in his troop. And Brad couldn't help wondering why the man was working with the girls. The excuse of doing it as a memorial to his wife sounded too good to be true.

"Mr. Deerling, we appreciate your taking this time to speak with us again," Gillian began.

Deerling waved away the words. "I'm going crazy over this. If there's anything I can tell you that will help, you can call me anytime, twenty-four, seven.''

Gillian met Brad's gaze then directed her words to Deerling. "Did Katie have any special friends in the group?''

"Everybody liked Katie. She's a sweet, friendly kid.'' He rubbed his forehead. "If I had to guess, I'd say maybe Karen Nichols. When we paired up for projects, they were usually together.''

Gillian scribbled the name in her notebook. "Any others?''

"Like I said, everyone liked Katie. The girls all go to the same school, so they see one another often.'' He frowned, the shallow lines around his mouth deepening. "I wish I knew something more. Maybe the girls will. I know it'll be difficult for them to talk about their friend, but they all want to help.''

Brad leaned forward. "Do you mind me asking, Mr. Deerling, why you're the troop leader?''

"Instead of a woman, you mean? It's no great mystery. All of the other girls' mothers work and didn't want to take on the responsibility.''

Brad wanted to compare Deerling's version to that of his sister-in-law's. "Yet you took it on, instead of your wife?"

Deerling's lips tightened. "My wife died six years ago. So it was me or no Scout troop for my daughters. It may be unconventional, but the other parents favored a male leader over having their girls miss out on Scouting altogether."

"It must be very difficult for you."

Deerling shrugged. "You do what you have to do."

Gillian looked up from her notes. "Do you have the list of the girls in the troop that I asked you for yesterday?"

Deerling reached for a paper on the side table. "I've listed phone numbers next to the names for you, too."

"Thank you," Gillian replied, accepting the paper. "You've been very thorough."

Brad watched the man closely. "How have the neighborhood searches gone?"

"Unfortunately, we haven't turned up anything. I'm afraid we're dealing with a very clever individual."

Maybe not. "Could you tell me again where you were when Katie was taken?"

Deerling glanced at Gillian. "I went over this yesterday."

"Just double-checking." Brad opened his notepad. "Sometimes even a remote fact becomes a clue."

"Of course. As I told Agent Kramer, I spent the evening at my sister-in-law's home."

"All evening?"

"Until about midnight. I didn't realize you knew exactly when Katie disappeared."

Brad stared at the man. Hard. "Are you sure it was midnight?"

"I didn't look at my watch, if that's what you mean. But the late news was coming on as I left."

Brad met Gillian's sharp gaze. That didn't jibe with Valerie Donnelly's story of videos until eleven.

Gillian rose from her chair. "We appreciate your time, Mr. Deerling."

"Please call if there's anything else I can do."

"We will," Brad replied, walking to the front door.

Once outside, the fresh air was welcome.

Gillian reached for the car door. "So who's going to say it?"

Brad shook his head. "The man should either be nominated for father of the year—"

"Or it's the best cover I've ever seen."

"And with all the neighborhood searches, if he did snatch her, then he has her hidden really well," Brad mused.

Gillian's expression was grim. "Or she's completely out of the area. Which leaves about a thousand places to search."

CHAPTER FOUR

THAT EVENING GILLIAN greedily drank her coffee, needing the caffeine pickup. It had been a long day. Dozens of interviews, as many dead ends. And the tension of working alongside Brad had manifested itself as a knot at the back of her neck.

She watched him now as he thanked the owner of the small grocery store where he'd left his car earlier in the day. The man had provided hot coffee to the police and searchers.

Gillian's cell phone rang. Reaching into her bag, she flipped it open and answered without losing a drop of coffee—a habit perfected out of necessity. She relaxed when she heard Teri's voice.

"What's up?" Gillian asked, feeling the coffee kick in. She wondered if there was a candy machine anywhere close.

"Just calling to see what time you're going to be at Mom and Dad's."

Gillian's mind was blank. "Mom and Dad's?"

"Gillian!" Teri's normally cheerful voice had gone big-sister stern in seconds. "I can't believe you forgot!"

Wincing, Gillian wondered if she dared ask what she'd forgotten.

Teri ended her dilemma. "I realize working with Brad has consumed most of your brain cells, but forgetting a family birthday!"

Her father's birthday, Gillian realized with dismay. Luckily she'd bought his gift weeks earlier.

"From the silence, I'm guessing you figured out whose birthday," Teri chided her. "Don't tell me you have to work."

"Couldn't you have reminded me today?"

"I didn't think I needed to."

"Ouch." Gillian studied Brad, biting down on her lip. "Would anyone care if I brought a straggler with me?"

Teri's sigh resonated over the wireless

connection. "What we *care* about is you. I don't suppose I should hold out any hope that the *straggler* is someone new and exciting?"

Gillian rolled her eyes.

"And don't roll your eyes," Teri said at nearly the same instant. "I suppose you want me to give the family a heads-up on this one."

"It wouldn't hurt." Gillian hesitated. "I have my reasons, you know."

"There's no talking you out of them, I'm sure." Teri sighed. "I just don't want to see you get hurt again."

"That's not going to happen."

"No one wishes that more than me," Teri told her. "But you don't know you like I do. You put your heart out there in the open, and it's just too tempting. It gets whacked to pieces every time."

"Now, that's quite an image," Gillian told her, hoping to lighten Teri's mood.

"You'll always be my little sister," Teri replied. "So I'll always worry about you. But if you want to bring Brad, that's okay, too."

"You won't tell everyone to be cool toward him?" Gillian asked anxiously, envisioning her plan crumbling before it was even completely formed.

Teri made an impatient noise on the other end. "You really have used up all your gray cells. *I* haven't lost sight of the fact that it's Dad's birthday. It's supposed to be a fun celebration, not a game of frozen statues."

Gillian felt a rush of relief. "Thanks, Teri. I know I sound like a maniac, but it's important. Please just trust me."

"As if I have a choice," Teri muttered.

"I'll try to be there by eight. And let Mom know we won't be able to stay long." Gillian saw that Brad had finished and was heading toward her. "I've got to run now." She flipped the phone closed.

"A new lead?" Brad asked, watching as she clipped the phone back on her belt.

"Not exactly. Tonight's a birthday dinner for my dad."

Brad glanced at his watch. "So you want to knock off early? I can follow up on my own tonight."

"That won't work."

He drew his brows together. "Why not?"

"Because you're going with me to the birthday dinner."

"Oh, no—" he began.

She held up her hand. "Before you say anything else—we'll keep our appearance brief so we can get back to work. And remember? It's part of our deal. I allow you to work the investigation. You come to family functions with me."

"Tonight?"

"Just when were you planning to make good on that part of the deal? Next Christmas?"

"It's too sudden," Brad protested.

"Fine. You stay off the investigation until my family plans something else."

Defeat warred with anger on his face.

And she experienced a sudden epiphany. "You didn't think you'd have to go through with your part of the agreement!"

"We can't just leave the investigation on hold."

"There are four detectives and a squadron of officers working the case. And right now I'm waiting on reports from the neighborhood canvassing before I can follow up on anything else. Next excuse?"

Reluctance clouded his features. "I suppose a deal's a deal."

Gillian glanced down at her dusty loafers. "I should go home and grab a shower."

"Yeah, me, too." He hesitated, flipping his keys, the sound of clinking metal the only one between them.

The pause was so long Gillian shifted her position against the car. She suddenly felt as though she had time-warped back to high school when she'd just asked a guy to the Sadie Hawkins dance and he'd agreed to go only because he couldn't get out of the invitation.

Brad pulled off his sunglasses. "What time are you supposed to be there?"

"Eight."

He glanced at his watch. "It only takes ten minutes to get to your parents' house...." He stopped himself. "Sorry. Forgot that was from our old place. I don't know where you live now."

"Not far from there," she managed to say, wincing inwardly at the mention of the home they had shared. "Fifteen minutes away now." To cover the reaction, she turned, scribbling her address and phone number on a sheet of paper, then ripping it free.

He accepted the note. "I'll pick you up at seven forty-five."

As she agreed, Gillian wondered if she'd made a very bad deal.

BRAD HADN'T BEEN BACK to this neighborhood since the divorce. Memories sprung from the most unlikely places. The park he and Gillian had gone for picnics wasn't a surprising trigger. But as he passed the video store, Brad remembered a night they'd walked there to rent a movie. It had begun raining as they strolled home. Gillian loved the rain, and she'd lifted her face to let it run over her cheeks. Soaked by the time they reached the apartment, it hadn't taken long for their wet bodies to come together, the video forgotten.

Theirs had been a mad, impulsive, passionate relationship. Optimistic and open, Gillian saw sunshine in the worst of days, light in the most difficult situation.

But Brad couldn't think like Gillian. He couldn't even imagine a life so textbook perfect. It was as though she and her family had remained untouched by sadness or mishap, certainly from any tragedy. And they all acted as though that were the norm. They didn't understand the darker side of life, the pain many people had to endure.

Brad left the main arterial road and drove down a residential street, seeing it through new eyes. He had blocked out how appealing this neighborhood was. Older homes surrounded by ancient, moss-draped oaks and wide, deep lawns contributed to the charm.

Having memorized Gillian's address, Brad searched for the apartment complex, thinking that one didn't really belong in this cozy area.

Then he saw it, tucked far back on a large lot, next to a widespread ranch house. It was a small complex. White brick arched walls were lit by tall gas carriage lights. A black wrought-iron gate provided a discreet entrance.

The place instantly reminded Brad of New Orleans. Tall palm trees grew close together, creating a thick-leaved lattice overhead. Honeysuckle vines crept over the top of a brick fence, intertwining with bougainvillea and ivy.

He parked, thinking it looked like the sort of place Gillian would choose, no sharp angles or aggressive chrome. As he walked through the gate he saw the banks of multipaned French windows. Yes, it was Gillian.

There couldn't be more than twenty units in the complex, and each one had a private courtyard. The cop part of him said the place was ideal for robbers and stalkers. But something inside said it was also perfect for romance. And that caused him to wonder if Gillian had found a new man.

Shaking off the thought, he strode to her apartment, clanging the brass knocker beside the French doors a bit harder than he'd intended. He heard a rustling at the doors before she pulled them open.

''Hi,'' she greeted him, her voice sounding softer than it had earlier that day. ''Come in. I'm almost ready. I just have to put on my earrings.''

She'd always left them for last. He swallowed. It was difficult to know such intimate details, yet pretend they were forgotten, that they had no impact on him.

She disappeared into what he guessed was the bedroom, leaving him to study her apartment. He could see that she'd chosen intriguing antique pieces, coupled with a comfortable-looking traditional couch. Warm and informal, nothing screamed "do not touch."

It suited her, Brad realized with surprise. When they had furnished their home, she had never voiced her apparent love of antiques when he'd told her he preferred contemporary furnishings.

"I'm ready."

He turned around, seeing that she looked more relaxed as she strolled toward him, holding a gift bag and her purse.

She paused next to him, looking up expectantly. An image of the days when they'd tumbled from bed still wanting more flashed through his mind. She would stand this close to him, and he would reach to cup his hand around the back of her neck, to pull her to him for a final kiss.

"Brad?" she asked, her dark eyes wide with questions, her unique scent drifting around him.

A trace of nerves played across her face as she tossed back her silky hair. It was the first time since they'd begun the investigation that he'd seen it loose.

"Are you ready?" She looked toward the door, a touch of anxiety in her voice.

Belatedly realizing he was blocking the way, Brad opened the door and then stepped aside, allowing Gillian to walk out ahead of him.

As they drove to her parents' house, Gillian was unusually quiet. He wondered if she remembered when it had been natural for them to be together. He couldn't seem to forget.

The driveway was filled with cars. Apparently every member of her family was in attendance. Brad parked on the street and allowed Gillian to take the lead as they walked toward the house. In the past, they'd entered through the back door—going straight into the family-friendly kitchen.

"Everyone's probably in the living

room,'' Gillian told him as they headed up the sidewalk to the front door. She didn't ring the bell. Theirs was a casual family. As Gillian's hand closed around the knob, she glanced back at Brad. ''You okay?''

And for that one moment he was. ''Yeah.''

Gillian held his gaze a touch longer, then pushed the door open. Chaos reigned. Kramer siblings, their spouses and a spattering of grandchildren all seemed to be speaking at once. There was so much activity that no one noticed them at first.

Suzanne, Gillian's mother, glanced up. For a moment she tensed, then rose, meeting them in the entry hall.

''Brad,'' she greeted him. ''It's been awhile.''

''Yes. Nice to see you.''

Her smile became warmer as she seemed to sense his hesitation. She linked her arm with his. ''Gillian should have told us sooner you were coming,'' she told him, her gaze chiding her youngest. ''But we're delighted to see you.''

''I hope I'm not intruding.'' Brad knew

he couldn't have felt more awkward if Gillian had paraded him buck-naked through the Kramer house.

"Of course not. We always have an extra seat at the table."

Brad caught sight of Gillian's father. Although everyone had been on civil terms during the divorce, Brad knew fathers felt especially protective toward their daughters.

But Frank was rising from his chair.

"Frank."

The elder Kramer extended his hand. "Brad."

As they shook hands, Brad marveled at the open, happy faces, so starkly different from his family.

Teri and David approached. Teri gave Brad a quick hug, surprising him yet again. And her husband offered his hand.

Gillian's brothers, Craig and Grant, approached a bit more slowly. Gillian was the baby sister in every sense. Although the men greeted him, Brad felt their reserve.

"We're having appetizers," Suzanne was telling him as they made their way deeper into the living room.

"The grandkids made them as a surprise. The peanut butter, marshmallow, Gummi Bear ones are their specialty," Frank added with a discreet expression of warning. "What are you drinking?"

Brad remembered that Frank was a connoisseur of fine Scotch. Since he was driving, that caused a twinge of regret. "Coffee. Black."

While Frank went to get his drink, Brad glanced at Gillian. But she wasn't paying attention to him. Instead she knelt to accept sticky kisses and heartfelt hugs from her nieces and nephews.

In the past, when visiting with Gillian's family, Brad had felt as though he'd been asked to eat dinner with the Waltons.

He had few such happy memories of his own family. There had been a time...but that was before Amanda vanished and the small family had been ripped apart. Since then, the good memories had almost completely faded under the strength of the bad.

Suzanne clapped her hands together to be heard above a half dozen overlapping conversations. "Let's head into the dining room."

Dreading the remainder of the evening, Brad swallowed a fortifying shot of strong coffee.

As he replaced his cup in its saucer, Suzanne took his elbow. "Why don't I run interference?"

Brad hoped his nervousness wasn't too obvious. "You think it'll be needed?"

But Suzanne only smiled gently. "You know what a mob we are, Brad."

He nodded, grateful that Suzanne was anything but the stereotypical mother-in-law.

She seated Brad next to a small boy. Teri sat on the other side of the child.

Her daughter, Rachel, was on her right. The five-year-old's face was bright with curiosity. "Mommy said you went away, Uncle Brad."

Clearing his throat, he looked at Teri for help, but her expression plainly said he was on his own. "That's true. I moved to the other side of town."

"How come?" Rachel persisted.

He settled for a neutral response. "My job is there."

Rachel considered this. To Brad's relief she moved on to another topic, pointing to the small boy seated next to him. "Can you tell which twin that is?"

From her eager face, Brad suspected this was a favorite game of hers. He turned to the boy. "I'm not sure."

She giggled, an impish sound. "Guess."

Brad cocked his head unable to distinguish between the boy and his twin. They'd changed a great deal since he'd last seen them.

Imitating Brad's motion, Rachel cocked her small head. "There's two of them, you know."

Brad raised his eyebrows in deliberate surprise. "Really?"

"That's what makes them twins," the child explained patiently. "You're 'pposed to know that. You're a grown-up."

Brad made a show of examining his large hands. "So I am."

Teri reached over, tugging gently on her

daughter. "That's enough, Rachel. You'll talk his ear off."

"Uh-uh," the child objected. "I don't know how."

"Not to worry," Teri responded. "You're getting the knack."

"It's okay," Brad told his former sister-in-law.

Teri met his eyes over the head of her precocious child. "We do our best to make sure unexpected guests are treated politely."

Unexpected guests. Teri was subtle, but Brad caught the subtext.

Gillian stood beside him suddenly, leaning to fill his water glass. "They're a tough crowd," she told him, her voice traveling to reach her sister.

Teri jerked her head up, a guilty look on her face. "Sorry," she muttered.

Brad kept his expression benign. "You've done nothing to apologize for."

"And nothing to boost the family pride, either," Gillian retorted, glaring at her sister.

Uncomfortably Brad straightened in his chair. "I don't want to spoil your father's party."

"You're not," Teri told him with a cheerfulness Brad couldn't call either true or false. "Dad always says the more the better. Don't let my lapse of manners ruin a perfectly lovely evening." She retrieved a napkin from one of her sons, who'd been busily trying to pull his place setting from the table. "We won't keep you in suspense any longer. This twin is Dallas."

Gillian leaned close enough so that Brad and Teri could hear, but so her voice didn't travel down the table. "As you know, we're lucky she didn't name the other one Fort Worth."

"Gill!" Teri protested. "You know it's a family name!"

Little Dallas didn't seem perturbed, having heard the jest before. Rachel, however, continued chattering. "That's silly, huh, Brad?"

"Sure is. I'd have named them Minneapolis and St. Paul."

"That sounds like a church name," Rachel replied with practical reasoning.

"So it does. Guess that's why I'm not in charge of choosing names."

"You have to have *babies* to get to name one," Rachel told him with exaggerated patience. "Didn't you know that?"

Brad looked at neither Gillian nor Teri. "Must have forgotten."

"That's okay," Rachel said, handing him a grape she'd filched from the table. "I forget stuff, too."

"Then I'm in good company," Brad managed to say.

As Gillian moved around the table filling goblets, young Rachel shifted a tad closer. "I have more grapes if you want some."

Was it an inborn Kramer trait, Brad wondered suddenly. To offer balm from childhood forward? "That's okay. I think we're going to start eating any minute."

Dallas sighed a sigh as big as he was. "It always takes *forever*."

Since it was feeling that way to Brad as well, he didn't disagree.

Gillian soon slipped into the chair beside him. "I think my mother planned to sit here, but I preempted her bid." She reached for her water. "I think she was afraid you'd be the main course, so she was trying to protect you.''

It was actually rather sweet, Brad realized. But he was out of touch with sweet familial moments. Uncomfortable, he sneaked a glance at his watch.

''We haven't even had salad,'' Gillian remarked in a quiet yet wry voice. ''It's going to be a long evening if you're already clocking off the minutes.''

''What makes you think it will go any faster if I don't?'' A flash of hurt crossed her face and inwardly he cursed his words. ''Gillian—''

''You're right, of course.'' Gillian smoothed the napkin in her lap. ''But luckily it looks as though we're about to begin.''

Feeling like a heel, Brad remained quiet.

The rest of the dinner passed uneventfully, but that didn't make him feel any better. A cake was brought out, and amid much laughter and encouragement candles were extinguished to spontaneous applause.

''Did you make a wish, Dad?'' Teri asked.

Frank glanced around the table, his gaze

resting on Suzanne. "Yep. And it's already come true."

His adult children tossed rumpled napkins in his direction.

Brad was uncomfortably aware of the pristine napkin that lay across his lap. The Kramers displayed their feelings like highway billboard signs. But he'd never been able to join in their uninhibited exchanges.

"Presents! Presents!" the grandchildren started to chant.

Frank rubbed his hands together, forgoing any false modesty. "I'll open the gifts if you agree to eat cake."

The children cheered for their grandfather, and even Brad found himself smiling. The old man had a way about him.

Remembering the gift in his pocket, Brad unobtrusively pulled it out, placing it at the side of the large mound of presents. Young Dallas followed his every move, his eyes widening when he saw the tissue-wrapped gift.

Seeing the child's mouth open to question it, Brad put a finger to his own lips. Delighted by the secret he shared, Dallas bounced up and down on the chair a bit but didn't say anything.

No persuasion was needed to dig into the rich, fudgy chocolate cake. It was Suzanne's specialty—and her family's favorite.

Brad was quiet, observing the members of the family as they enjoyed their father, the cake, one another. Exclamations punctuated the animated conversation as the gifts were opened.

When Frank came to Brad's present, he paused, not seeing a card. Looking intrigued, he pulled open the tissue paper. Surprise stilled his movements as he revealed the brilliant paperweight.

He glanced down the length of the table, obviously wondering who the gift was from. "This is incredible. Who…?" Frank asked, glancing from face to face.

Before the moment became awkward, Brad cleared his throat to speak.

But Dallas could keep his secret no longer. "It's from Brad!"

Every head at the table swung in his direction.

Brad resisted the urge to squirm under their inspection. "Happy birthday, Frank."

Frank removed the paperweight from its tissue-paper nest and held it up. Light from the chandelier bounced off the prism, reflecting the colors of a cut diamond rather than the expected rainbow. "I don't know what to say, Brad. This is...well, a piece of art."

"I collect art glass," Brad explained, having seen the questions on Gillian's face, knowing she was wondering where he'd obtained the piece on such short notice. "And I know you collect paperweights. It seemed a good combination."

"If this is part of your collection, I can't accept it!" Frank protested.

"It would please me for you to have it." The older man had always treated him squarely, despite the outcome of his marriage to Gillian.

Frank ran an appreciative finger over the enticing object. "It *would* be the most unique one I own."

"Enjoy it, Frank," Brad told him. "Half the pleasure I take in this hobby comes from acquiring the pieces. Now I have a good excuse to add another one.''

''Thank you, Brad. I'll enjoy it.''

Just then Gillian's cell phone rang. Pulling it from her belt, she listened for a few moments.

''I'll be right on it,'' she said into the phone before flipping it shut. Then she glanced at her parents. ''Sorry, Dad, Mom. I've got to run.''

Her mother stood with Gillian and Brad. ''We understand, dear.''

''We'll walk you to the door,'' Frank added.

In the front entry hall, Suzanne hugged Brad lightly. ''It was lovely having you, dear.''

''Thank you for dinner, Suzanne. That cake of yours is still wicked.''

Pleased, she smiled. ''Don't be a stranger.''

Brad glanced at Gillian, not sure just how long he was to be included in the Kramer family gatherings. ''Thanks.''

Frank shook his hand. ''Can't thank you

enough for the paperweight, Brad. It'll be the jewel of my collection.''

Brad nodded. Then he and Gillian were outside. Breathing deeply of the night air, he turned to her. ''Where are we off to?''

''*I'm* headed to check out a lead in Galveston.''

Automatically he gripped her arm. ''Not by yourself.''

She glanced down at his restraining hand, her voice deadly calm. ''We're not married anymore, Brad.''

He bit back a curse. ''I'm not trying to control you. This isn't Dodge City, and you don't need to be charging off fifty miles away in the middle of the night by yourself. I'm offering to be backup, unless your partner's available.''

She fiddled with her purse. ''He's not. And I don't want to wait until he's free. Dispatch said it was urgent.''

Brad pulled the keys from his pocket. ''Not to mention *I'm* driving.''

She stopped short at the words.

He hid a smile. ''I wondered when you'd remember you didn't have your car here.''

"YOU SURE THIS IS IT?" Brad asked skeptically once they'd located the address in Galveston.

Gillian looked at the dark house, reserving her own doubts. "It checks against the anonymous tip Dispatch gave me."

"It doesn't smell right," Brad muttered.

Gillian agreed, but she didn't want to take the position of weak female with Brad. She'd seen much scarier locales in her time with the agency. "You can stay here if you'd like."

"Funny."

Together they eased from the car, mutely agreeing to remain quiet since the place suggested caution. Although there was only a sliver of moonlight, the house seemed unnaturally dark. From all the overgrown foliage, Gillian guessed. Its thickness seemed to choke the shingled exterior of the small place, capturing any light.

A screen door, an island necessity, sagged limply against the front door. Pushing it aside, Gillian searched for a doorbell. Not finding one, she pounded on the sturdy wood. The sound seemed unnatural in the night.

"Dead-end street," Brad observed. "Only one way out of here."

Gillian felt tension settle in at the back of her neck. Consciously she straightened to her full height and knocked again, despite the cobwebs covering the jamb.

But nothing stirred in the house or the deserted yard.

Brad flipped open the mailbox, pulling out some yellowed circulars. "I think the place is empty. Doesn't seem like the electricity is on and there's no current mail."

Gillian nodded in agreement. "Let's check all the entry points to see if the cobwebs have been disturbed."

They scanned the back door and all the windows of the single story house. The intact grime and cobwebs assured them the house hadn't been entered. These coastal houses had no basement that could be concealing little girls.

Brad directed the beam of his flashlight over the nearly obscured house numbers.

"We could check it out in the daylight tomorrow."

"Yeah. We won't be able to see much tonight." She scratched her head, thinking aloud. "Funny. It almost seems like a tactic to distract us from our case, but it's pretty much a wasted effort since we don't have a single real lead."

Brad continued surveying the house. "Maybe someone thinks we do."

Gillian couldn't prevent her shudder. It wasn't like her. She'd been on plenty of dangerous assignments before.

Brad seemed to catch her sense of discomfort. "Let's get out of here."

Gillian didn't disagree. There was something unnerving in the air.

Once inside the SUV, she sneaked a look at Brad, but he looked neither smug nor condescending. More troubling, he looked perturbed. "Brad?"

He glanced at her as he drove away from the house, heading toward the ocean. "Why don't we get some coffee before we drive back to the city?"

The coffee might ease the chill she felt. "Sure."

Within a few minutes, they were on the highway fronting the seawall. Cars cruised the popular street that was lined with restaurants and attractions. Gillian wondered which place Brad would choose.

When he turned into a hamburger drive-through, she couldn't prevent a small snort. "The deluxe treatment, eh?"

He rolled down his window, ordering two large cups of coffee. "I thought we could take them down to the beach."

Her throat clogged as memories overtook her, memories of their time spent on that very beach. So much in love, all they'd needed was a bit of sand and each other.

"That okay?" Brad was asking.

She hoped her voice wouldn't sound as raw as her emotions. "Sure."

It didn't take long to find a parking space. Midweek, the beach wasn't as crowded as it would be when the tourists flocked there on the weekend. They walked down the steep steps of the tall seawall that curved along the length of the sand and protected the Victorian town.

The wall made the beach seem very private, buffering it from the crowds above. Traffic sounds dimmed. Only the lapping of the incoming tide and breaking waves filled the air.

Gillian breathed in the unmistakable smells of seaweed and hemp. To her it was an intoxicating mixture that beckoned the past. Growing up in Houston, she had fond memories of family days spent in Galveston, since it was their favorite place to picnic, swim and sun. As an adult, she had even more special memories spent with Brad. One of her keenest regrets was that the two had never entwined. Perhaps if they had, Brad could have learned the joy, rather than the pain, of having a family.

Impulsively she kicked off her shoes, reaching to pick them up. "I can't resist digging my toes in the sand."

His chuckle was quiet. "Ah, the power of the sea."

She murmured agreement, then took a

deep breath. "The gift you gave Dad—it was very thoughtful."

He shrugged. "It seemed to suit him."

Gillian visualized the exquisite paperweight. "You didn't have to, though."

"Yeah. I did."

She digested that comment, taking a quick peek at him. There was such strength in his features. It was something she had been attracted to the first time she'd met him. She had been so idealistic, so hopeful.

"Penny for your thoughts," Brad commented, bringing her back to the present.

"They're worth at least a nickel," she replied, sharing a smile with him. Then, afraid to let that grow, she stubbed a toe into the soft sand. "When did you start collecting art glass?"

A strange expression crossed his face.

"Did I say something wrong?" she asked, wondering what he so quickly hid.

"No. It's hard to explain. But I should qualify my *collection*. It's not exactly Smithsonian-size. I was attracted to a piece, and for a long time I had just the one. I have only a few more now."

Inexplicably touched, she caught his arm. "Yet you gave one to Dad."

He met her eyes. "I owed him."

She swallowed, afraid to speak, afraid to look away, afraid not to do either.

Irrationally, Gillian wished she could turn back the clock, forget what had torn them apart.

The water, inching closer with the tide, lapped at her feet, dampening the ankles of her pants. She was glad for the warm rush of seawater, which made her realize what she'd just wished.

Together, they stepped away from the water.

Gillian shook her pants legs. "I'm probably full of sand. How about you? Did you get wet?"

"Not enough to matter." He glanced down at her pants. "You'll dry."

She shook the fabric more vigorously. "How gallant."

A sudden whizzing sound erupted beside her. Before she could react, Brad tackled her face first into the sand.

Brad rolled on top of her, ending her efforts to rise. "Stay still," he said quietly.

"Bullet?" she questioned as best as she could with no room to move her mouth.

"I'm not sure." His voice was grim and she imagined he was surveying the area.

She pushed at his weight. "If you get off me, I can be an asset instead of a liability."

He hesitated, then moved to one side.

Gillian swiped at the sand on her face, then reached for the gun in her shoulder holster. "Can you see anything?"

"No."

For a few moments, Gillian studied the shadowy formations surrounding them. Rocks, she knew. But in the dark, they were menacing.

Stiffening, she saw a set of figures coming toward them. "Brad…"

"I see them," he responded shortly.

Gillian held her breath, tightening the grip on her gun.

"Kids," Brad said suddenly.

She lowered her gun, seeing what he did. Three teenagers were throwing bottles at the rocks. The explosion of glass was unnerving, but innocuous.

The chill she'd felt earlier returned and the pleasure of the beach dimmed. Brad stood quickly and she accepted his outstretched hand. Brushing sand from her clothes, Gillian also tried to brush away the remnants of the sensation she'd felt when Brad's body had been so close.

As they climbed back to the car, Gillian wondered what she was doing there with her ex-husband. And why she kept giving in to him.

CHAPTER FIVE

BRAD WAS ON EDGE the following morning. Armed with a strong cup of coffee, he was waiting for Gillian to meet him after her daily briefing with the team.

Seeing her push open the glass door to the small café, he studied her carefully. Gillian's skin looked paler than usual, her eyes shadowed. He wondered if her sleep had been as disturbed as his.

As she slid into the booth, he poured a second mug of coffee from the pot the waitress had left earlier. "What did the others think about the deserted house in Galveston?"

Instead of answering, she picked up her mug, taking a healthy swallow without adding her usual cream.

"Gillian?"

"We don't know that it's related to the case."

"And what if it is?"

"I should have waited for my partner, instead of letting you ride along."

"I watched your back. What more could your partner have done?"

She set her lips in an uncompromising line of silence.

"Gillian?"

"I don't want a bodyguard," she told him flatly.

His gut tightened at the thought of what could have happened to her if she'd been on her own. "Maybe you need one."

"In case it hasn't occurred to you, if either the agency or HPD assigns someone to me, then you're out of the picture."

He sucked in a deep breath of frustration. "I don't want you getting hurt."

"But you *do* want to be in on the investigation," she responded. Before he could retort, she held up a hand. "I'm not suggesting that you're willing to put me out to dry to get your own way, but think about it. What would we accomplish? I don't have an established record with my new boss. He might yank me. You'll definitely be side-lined. And then what? The case starts over again with a new lead? Then we lose the time we've already put in.''

Brad knew she was right. ''I still don't like it.''

''That's okay. You've rarely liked the way I do things.''

He rubbed his temples, feeling the beginnings of a headache. God, she was stubborn. ''You aren't going to give in on this, are you?''

''I never have on the important issues,'' she reminded him.

It might be a migraine before the day was over. ''Did you come up with anything new in the briefing?''

She shook her head. ''Still no ransom demands. The only tangible lead is the Scout leader and we don't have anything else on him yet.''

He nodded. ''Do you want to watch him?''

''Yes, I've taken the first shift.'' She glanced at her watch. ''Until around noon.

Galveston PD said they ought to have something for us by then on the ownership of the house.''

Brad nodded. What really disturbed him was the possibility that someone had watched them at the deserted house, then tailed them to the beach. Brad had the chilling suspicion that they were being toyed with. And since Gillian, not him, was linked to the case, that meant *she* was the one being watched.

She took another sip of coffee. ''I've had enough caffeine to fuel me for the day.''

He pushed his own mug toward the center of the table. ''I'm ready.''

The morning passed quickly. Mark Deerling proved to be a boring subject. After a morning's surveillance, they'd learned that the man went on his coffee break with several office mates and that he had a soft spot for doughnuts.

''I don't want to say this has been a waste—'' Brad began.

''But it has,'' Gillian finished for him. She glanced at her watch. ''I'll assign someone to keep him under surveillance for the rest of our shift. Let's bag this and head for Galveston.''

''We may be early for the locals, but we could make up for skipping breakfast by grabbing some seafood.''

Although Interstate 45 South was always busy, it was well before rush hour and they made good time, leaving the big city behind them before too long. Although the area was developed completely between Houston and its smaller neighbor, the topography differed.

Tall, sparse grasses grew in the loamy soil, the stalks bending in the strong winds that came ashore with the tides. Houses built on stilts occupied both the marshes and the high ground.

Reaching the Causeway bridge that was the only southern land route from the mainland to the island, they joined the line of cars. The Galveston Island had been over-built since the sixties. If another large hurricane struck, it would be impossible for the entire population to evacuate in time. Which, in Brad's estimation, made the island a nice place to visit rather than live.

The concrete bridge was two miles long, but they were eventually across and on to the island. Tall oleander bushes lined the streets, their fuchsia blooms ruffling in the breeze.

The sun was high, banishing the remnants of the previous evening's chill. Seagulls dove in lazy abandon at specks of food while wide-jawed pelicans shook their jowls and strolled the boardwalk. Stone jetties broke up the endless ocean. Commercial piers were built on some of them, but none were crowded.

Brad took a familiar road, but one off the beaten track. They passed the burned-out ruins of what had once been Jean Lafitte's settlement. The base for the infamous pirate's operation had contained huts for the pirates, a shipyard, pool halls and Lafitte's own mansion, the Maison Rouge. He was forced to flee the area after attacking an American ship in 1821, but first he burned the settlement to the ground. Many locals still believed the tales of his buried treasure, but it had never been found.

Despite the lure of Lafitte and his treasure,

few tourists ventured in to the area since it was well beyond the popular Strand. They crossed railroad tracks and went past an oyster-processing plant, turning on to a narrow road that ran alongside the waterfront.

Brad eventually stopped in the lot of a nondescript restaurant. After shutting off the engine he glanced at Gillian.

Recognition filled her face. ''Oyster po'boys,'' she breathed.

He smiled, remembering how she loved this place, which they had discovered when they were dating. Despite all the first-class, five-star restaurants on the island, they had always gravitated here. Favored by the locals it was both unpretentious and fast. They would be in and out quickly. As he opened his door, Brad hoped it wasn't a mistake to choose a place they had shared.

''Is this okay?''

But Gillian was too practical to overreact. ''You're right. This place is the best.''

Once inside, they were seated next to the huge wall-size window that overlooked the bay. Shrimp boats docked just outside the window, their tall masts a webbed procession in the sun-washed sky.

"Looks like some of the boats just brought in a fresh catch," Gillian mused, as they watched icehouses being filled with the squirming loads.

Birds, emboldened by habit, tried to steal what they could of the new catch. Batted away, they returned time and again. One fisherman threw a fish at the birds and they neglected the shrimp for the new feast. Smaller birds trailed their bigger, bolder cousins, looking for scraps.

"It never changes," Brad remarked, looking at one particularly brazen bird that refused to be intimidated by the fishermen. "I could swear that same bossy bird was here last time."

"He probably was," Gillian agreed, looking more relaxed than she had since they'd begun the case. "I like that it's the same. Birds diving and fussing. Ships looking sturdy and unsinkable. It looks so normal, unchangeable."

"You sound introspective."

She made circles in the drops of condensation on her iced tea glass. "Maybe. I don't know. I'd rather remember Galveston like this than…"

The past rose up again between them. "I know, Gillian."

She bit her lip, a habit he remembered well.

As he watched her, Brad thought of her willingness the previous night to go to the house alone. "Gillian, you can't take risks like you were prepared to last night."

Gillian leaned across the table. "Brad, you know the inherent danger of the job. We all accept it."

But he had never accepted it where Gillian was concerned. It shouldn't matter as much now, but it did.

Their food arrived, but Brad wasn't hungry any longer.

"Something wrong with your sandwich?" Gillian asked after a few minutes. "You're not eating."

He shrugged. "Just rethinking the case."

She lowered her half-eaten sandwich. "Brad, working together is bringing up too much history. As much as you want to be part of the investigation, perhaps you shouldn't continue.''

''And let you go off alone? You'll be a target.''

''I can ask for help from the team.''

He suspected she would be more comfortable with one of the others. But he wouldn't be. He doubted anyone else would take the need to protect her as seriously, certainly not as personally. ''Relax, Gillian. Things are just taking a different slant, one I wasn't expecting.''

''I have to know you're okay about the way I'm handling the case. Otherwise we can't work effectively.''

Brad knew he had two choices. He picked the only one he could live with. He lied. ''I can deal with it.''

She studied him for several moments, and he knew she wasn't certain whether or not to believe him. ''You're so sure?''

Casually he picked up the forgotten sandwich, needing the prop to appear convincing. ''As you said, it's part of the job.''

She lowered her eyes, picking at her French fries.

Although he forced himself to finish his lunch, Brad noticed that Gillian toyed with the remainder of hers. And though the simple charm of the setting hadn't changed, it was no longer comfortable. Both the past and the present had intruded on the moment.

After leaving the restaurant, they didn't take long to reach the house.

Gillian climbed from her side of the car, staring across the yard. "It doesn't seem as menacing in the daylight."

"You didn't mention 'menacing' last night."

"You didn't seem in the mood to hear it."

So he hadn't. He walked to the front of the house, peering into the dirty windows.

"Any sign of recent occupation?"

"No. The dust is thick, undisturbed."

She glanced downward. "And the ground's hard—we haven't had rain in more than a week. There won't be any clear footprints."

By silent consent they walked toward the rear of the house. The yard was completely overgrown. It looked as though it hadn't seen a mower in months.

Brad paused, gesturing ahead. Amid the thick tangle, a small hole had been pushed through the ivy lattice that led to the backyard.

"Do you see any other way to get back there?" Gillian asked, her voice lowered.

"Doesn't look like it. Let's circle back and see."

There was no alternative entrance.

Brad scanned the area, looking for trouble. "Someone's definitely been here."

Gillian nodded. "Of course it could be someone legitimate—the owners, or a maintenance person."

His gaze was skeptical. "Let's see if he left a calling card."

After an hour of careful searching, Gillian was fuming. "Not a cigarette butt or gum wrapper. Whoever was here was meticulous."

Their eyes met. That fit with their kidnapper.

Gillian reached for her phone. "I'll get a crime-scene unit over here."

Brad doubted it would do any good. Gillian was quiet as they left the house and drove toward the freeway.

When she did finally speak, her words jarred him. "Why would someone give us a tip about a deserted house? There's no reason to think the girls were being kept here."

"Maybe that was just to check you out," Brad replied, wishing again that the media hadn't provided Gillian's name in items about the kidnapping. She'd been interviewed the first day and her face had appeared on television and in the newspapers.

"That could be a good thing."

He turned to stare at her. "Are you nuts?"

"Maybe he likes to toy with his victims," Gillian mused.

Brad hated the cold knot of dread that developed as she voiced his theory. But it fit the profile the bureau had drawn up on the kidnapper. "An even better reason for you to keep your head down."

"That's exactly what I'm *not* going to do."

The cold settling over him was at odds with the warm day. "What are you saying?"

"That we've had nothing on the perp, no way to rescue the girls. Until now. If he'll come out of hiding to follow me, we could have our first break."

Terror, unlike any he'd experienced in his career, gripped him. "Gillian, you can't use yourself as bait."

She caught his gaze, her mahogany eyes glowing in the midday sunlight. "And if it were you? Would you walk away, knowing you'd possibly cheated these children out of their only chance?"

Brad cursed briefly, knowing his answer. Worse, Gillian knew as well.

BY THE TIME THEY RETURNED to Houston, Gillian had some preliminary news on the house in Galveston. The place had been empty for years. No utilities were connected, nor had much maintenance been performed. It belonged to an estate. The owners, an old couple who paid the taxes, hadn't been in the place for years. They were keeping it for a nephew who might or might not decide to live there someday. It was too run-down to currently be habitable. The nephew lived in Florida, but no one had been able to reach him.

Interviews hadn't gone well, either. Another trip to Deerling hadn't yielded anything. Parents of Katie's friends were eager to help but knew nothing.

Hours later, Brad glanced at his watch and swore under his breath when he saw that it was after eight o'clock.

Gillian pushed at the hair around her face, the humidity of the day taking its toll. "What is it?"

"I didn't realize it was so late."

"Plans?"

"Dinner with my parents. But I'll cancel—I'm already late."

"You don't have to cancel. Go ahead. I can take it from here."

"Alone?"

"Brad, in case you haven't noticed, no one's attempted anything."

He tried to hold his temper, but frustration spilled into his words. "Let's not argue the point. I'll call my parents and let them know I'm not coming.''

Snapping open his cell phone, he was surprised when Gillian placed her hand over his, blocking access to the number pad.

''You should see your parents. I'll be fine on my own.''

''No way.''

Surprise made her draw back. ''You can't shadow my every move.''

''Until we're sure why you were led to that deserted house, that's exactly what I plan to do.''

Her expression grew incredulous. ''In order to guard me, you're going to disappoint your parents?''

He brushed away the words. ''Not a big deal.''

Gillian shrugged. ''If that's the case, why not take me along instead of canceling?''

Startled, he studied her expression. ''Why do you want to go?''

''What a gracious invitation.''

''Sorry, that's not what I meant. I'm sure they'd like to see you. But—''

''If you think you can ditch this visit, then

follow me, you're nuts. It's your choice. We can go there and you can keep your watchful eye on me, or I go it alone. And trust me, I can lose you faster than a kid loses his homework.''

Exasperated, Brad wondered how so much stubbornness had been poured into such a small package. Realizing he wasn't going to win this one, he threw up his hands. ''Fine. We'll do it your way.''

She smiled, that sleek, satisfied smile he'd once relished.

Retrieving his cell phone, he called his parents, to tell them to eat without him. He also warned them the visit would be abbreviated due to work. His mother was delighted over the prospect of seeing her former daughter-in-law. Brad wished he could say he was delighted by the thought of bringing Gillian to see his parents again.

GILLIAN WAS UNACCOUNTABLY nervous as they drove to Brad's parents' home. She hadn't seen Elizabeth or Thomas Mitchell since the divorce. They'd been stricken by the action, obviously hurt over the loss of another family member.

The Mitchells had been a family in crisis. Even though they had lost Amanda sixteen years ago, the pain remained immediate. It was something Gillian had lived with on a daily basis when she and Brad had been married.

On more than one occasion he'd pointed out that she'd never had a loss, and therefore couldn't understand how he felt.

He was wrong, but only because she hadn't told him about what had happened to her in college. She'd had a brief affair that had resulted in a pregnancy during her senior year. She'd gone into premature labor late in her fifth month, and her tiny son had lived only a few hours.

Gillian had never said anything to Brad because she hadn't wanted him to agree to have a baby out of pity. Although, she'd never stopped hoping he would come to want a baby on his own.

Despite the secrets and their differences, they had loved each other, but Gillian couldn't give up on the idea of having a baby. Brad wouldn't budge, either, and eventually their childless marriage had ended.

However Gillian had never put any of the Mitchells out of her mind, always wishing she could do something, anything to help them move on. She wanted Brad to be happy, even if that meant he was apart from her.

Nervously adjusting her jacket, Gillian wondered if she would find the Mitchells unchanged, as though not a single page in the calendar had turned.

The door opened before they could knock, and Gillian realized the Mitchells must have been watching for them.

"Gillian!" Elizabeth cried, rushing forward, her hug warm and welcoming.

Incredibly touched, she returned the hug.

"What a wonderful surprise!" Elizabeth continued, finally releasing Gillian.

Brad's father, Thomas, hugged her as well. "My dear, you've stayed away too long."

"It's so good to see both of you," Gillian responded, realizing how true it was. Although their pain had scarred Brad, they had been nothing but kind and generous toward her.

Elizabeth chattered nonstop as she led the way into the cherry-wood-paneled den.

"Tell me what you've been up to," Elizabeth said, once they were settled in cozy chairs.

Seeing their expectant faces, Gillian felt a tad like a Santa Claus who had arrived without the expected presents. "Well, I've been working quite a bit. In fact, that's how Brad and I ran into each other."

"Stands to reason," Thomas replied. "Both of you in law enforcement."

"What kind of case are you working on?" Elizabeth asked. "It must be something big if it involves the police and the FBI."

Brad and Gillian exchanged glances.

"We can't really discuss it, Mom. It's an ongoing investigation."

The pleasure in her face dimmed. "Sounds dangerous."

Gillian's compassion spilled over, knowing how Brad's job worried them. "Not really. It's just a matter of protocol, so to speak, between the locals and the feds.''

Elizabeth, a sharp woman, didn't look completely convinced, but she did look as though she wanted to be.

''Whatever the reason, we're glad it brings you back here,'' Thomas told her.

Gillian smiled in return, wishing for the thousandth time that these people hadn't been subjected to so much pain.

''I kept the roast and mashed potatoes warm, if you're hungry.'' Elizabeth started to rise.

Fueled by the need to get back to the case, they waved away the offer.

''Fine, but I'm sending home plates. Brad lives on fast food and frozen dinners. I doubt he sees a vegetable unless he's here.''

As they talked, Gillian guessed the situation hadn't changed since she had seen them last—the Mitchells rarely had company. Their social life had ended all those years before and had never been repaired.

The loss was all around them, in the aging but touching possessions of Amanda's that still held prominence in the house. Brad had admitted that the memories associated with the house had made his parents consider a move, but they never could, worried that Amanda would come here and be unable to find them. Like many parents whose child was never found, the Mitchells had clung to the hope that someday she would return. The house had become their prison. They no longer subscribed to the newspaper and rarely watched the news.

Elizabeth smiled at them both. "If you won't eat dinner, how about some strudel?"

"No, thanks, Mom. I told Dad I'd take a look at the table saw."

"Brad's the only one who can keep that monster tamed," Thomas agreed. "But we don't have to do it tonight since Gillian's here."

"Don't mind me," Gillian responded quickly. "I'm sure Brad would like to take a look at your newest project."

Thomas seemed surprised. "You remember my woodworking?"

"Who could forget? You've made some incredible pieces."

Thomas waved away the compliment. "Just my puttering. But I enjoy it."

And it was all he had to distract himself, Gillian knew.

As the men left, Elizabeth rose. "I don't want to forget your doggie bags." However, her face was pensive, her mind obviously not on food.

"Is something wrong?"

Elizabeth lifted her gaze. "The case you and Brad are working on, it's the little girl who disappeared, isn't it?"

Gillian stiffened. Keeping the media under control was a difficult chore in a case that captured the public's attention. She and Brad had argued about further publicizing the case. Gillian believed additional publicity could keep the perp from snatching more children. Brad believed exactly the opposite. He feared the publicity would scare the kidnapper into getting rid of the victims.

Frowning, she wondered if he had talked about the case with his parents. "You know we're not supposed to discuss—"

"Ongoing investigations, I know. I'm right, though, aren't I?"

Reluctantly Gillian nodded.

"When I saw that little girl's picture posted at the grocery store, it brought everything back," Elizabeth confessed. "It's all I've thought about."

"Elizabeth, stop me if I'm interfering, but have you considering counseling?"

"Yes. We tried, but it didn't help."

"Wasn't that years ago?" Gillian probed gently.

"It was when Amanda...when she disappeared."

"Perhaps, since so many years have passed, it might turn out differently this time."

"Counseling," Elizabeth murmured. "I don't know. It seemed to make everything that much more painful."

"What about a support group?" Gillian suggested. "There are general grief groups and ones specifically for parents who have lost a child."

Elizabeth swallowed visibly. "It sounds so final that way. As though it's time to give up what hope is left."

Gillian clasped Elizabeth's shaking hands.

"Actually, it's just the opposite. From what you've all told me, Amanda was a kind and caring girl. I'm sure she wouldn't want you to go on suffering."

A spark brightened Elizabeth's eyes. "Amanda was incredibly thoughtful for one so young. Always bright and full of laughter."

"And you could share that with other parents, help them as well as yourselves."

"I never thought about it that way," Elizabeth responded slowly. "I guess we've always thought of ourselves as alone. I know many children die, but not to know seemed so much worse. I really can't say now which would be better."

"Either way, you and Thomas need to begin the healing process, to learn to enjoy the things you left behind."

Elizabeth glanced down. "I didn't realize it showed."

How could it not? "I know a psychologist from the bureau who can guide you to the right group."

"So many years," Elizabeth mused. "They've all run into one another. Yet, each day stands out separately, the inescapable conclusion once the night ends that Amanda hasn't come home again.''

Gillian hugged her former mother-in-law, feeling the contained sobs in her thin body. "That's why you have to get some help.''

Elizabeth withdrew finally, swiping at her eyes. "Perhaps you're right. Do you suppose that's why you've come back into our lives?''

Gillian wasn't certain, only that she wanted to help all of them.

Elizabeth fixed her with a steady gaze. "Whatever the reason, I'm glad you're back.''

Accepting another hug, Gillian didn't quash the hope glimmering in Elizabeth's eyes. Or the ridiculous bit in her own heart.

CHAPTER SIX

As HE DROVE HER HOME, Brad wondered if taking Gillian to his parents' house had been a mistake. He'd glimpsed the traces of tears in his mother's eyes. And when he'd questioned them, both she and Gillian had given him no real answers.

Glancing over at Gillian, Brad saw that she was idly studying the rush of cars still on the road even though it was after eleven. Houston didn't ever slow down. At least not visibly. Much like Gillian herself.

She turned just then, the deep brown of her eyes as dark as the night itself. "Not far now."

Brad switched his attention back to the traffic, knowing it was too dangerous to dwell on Gillian for many reasons. A few blocks later he turned on the inconspicuous road that led to her neighborhood.

She seemed surprised when he parked and got out of the car.

"There's no need to walk me to my door," she protested.

Once again Brad was struck by the impression that Gillian's courtyard would make a perfect place for someone to hide. "It's part of the service."

She shifted the plastic-wrapped plate of food Elizabeth had insisted on sending home with her. "I wonder how old we have to be before our parents are convinced we're capable of feeding ourselves."

"At least sixty. I noticed you didn't complain when Mom put in an extra slice of strudel."

Gillian sighed. "It's heaven on a plate." She reached for the wrought-iron handle of the gate.

Brad snagged her hand. "Did you leave the gate open?"

"I'm not sure." She shook away his arm. "What difference does it make?"

Exasperation gripped him. "Gillian, you're a cop. Don't close your eyes just because you're at home."

Practiced eyes studied the terrace. "I don't see anything out of place. I'm not concerned about the gate because a neighbor may have dropped by and not shut it securely when she left. That's happened before. It doesn't compromise the lock on the door."

The white wooden shutters on the ceiling-to-floor windows appeared undisturbed, as were the lacy curtains on the French doors. But that was no guarantee. "Let's make sure."

She stooped to deposit the food on a round patio table.

Brad hoped he was mistaken about the uneasy feeling he was experiencing. But that didn't deter him from checking his gun.

Gillian reached out before he could, testing the handle on her front door. It didn't turn. "It's secure. Just a false alarm."

Brad wasn't convinced. "Let's go inside. Make sure."

She rolled her eyes, then reached into her purse for the key. "I think it's overkill, but all right."

Brad was close behind her as Gillian

flipped on the lights in her living room. He scrutinized the area, but wasn't familiar enough with it to be certain if anything had been disturbed.

Gillian walked through the room confidently, glancing from side to side. She paused suddenly.

When she didn't stir, Brad moved to her side. "What is it?"

"Let's check the rest of the apartment."

Reflexively, Brad reached for his gun, noting that Gillian had drawn hers, as well. Apparently something was out of order.

It took only a few minutes to determine that the apartment was empty. All of the rooms looked neat, tidy, untouched. But Gillian wasn't given to panic. If she'd noticed something, it was genuine.

Regrouping in the living room, Brad watched Gillian walk over to her desk. She didn't touch anything, but instead studied the surface.

"What is it?" he asked.

"Something's gone."

He stepped nearer. "Do you know what?"

"My journal."

"Journal?"

"A diary of sorts."

"Are you sure it's not in one of the drawers? Maybe you tucked it away without realizing it."

A strange expression crossed her face. "No, I'm very certain."

"Did it contain anything valuable?"

The callousness of his words didn't hit until she raised offended eyes. "Put that way, I suppose not."

"Sorry, that's not what I meant. Did the journal contain any information another party would consider worth stealing?"

Slowly she shook her head. "No. Just my personal thoughts, observations."

The unease that had stricken him in the courtyard returned. This time it made the hair on the back of his neck rise. "Observations?"

She shrugged. "Ones that have no use to anyone but me."

"Not even to our perp?"

Gillian narrowed her eyes. "That's a pretty big leap."

"Luring you to a deserted house, then taking your diary—an instruction manual on how to get inside your head—is not a leap."

"We don't know this has anything to do with the case."

Brad wasn't certain he really wanted to hear the answer to his next question. "Does anyone have a key to your apartment?"

"There's a spare at my parents, and Teri has the other."

"You'd better check on both."

"Brad, I don't think—"

"If this were a case you were working, what would you do?"

She picked up the phone. Within a few minutes she confirmed that no one in her family had used the keys.

That left them with the question of how someone had broken in. Gillian was savvy enough to have installed superior-quality locks on her doors and all were intact. Which meant the intruder was smart.

"We should call CSU, see if he got careless, left a fingerprint." Brad knew it had to be done even though it would mean the end to his participation in the case.

"I doubt there's anything here." Yet she opened the closet and pulled out a box. "I have a kit. I'll dust the desk and door, but I'll bet the only prints there are mine."

She was wrong, though. Brad's prints showed up as well.

He was surprised. "It seems that you ought to have more prints—your family, neighbors, even the maintenance personnel."

"True. But my weekly cleaning lady came today. She always wipes everything down. I'm not saying there's not an odd print here or there, but she has a thing about germs and she washes all the trim, light switches, doorknobs, phones, that sort of thing."

"And the theft occurred on the one day your cleaning lady was here," Brad mused. "So, if you reported the break-in, it would be understandable that your apartment has no fingerprints other than your own. Or mine."

Gillian strolled to the windows, checking the locks for the third time. "It doesn't make sense," she muttered.

"Whoever did this is unaccustomed to making mistakes. I suspect the gate was left slightly ajar only because someone came by. If we hadn't noticed the gate, you might not have realized immediately that your journal was gone." An unwanted thought hit him. "It could have been returned later without your noticing."

"In the middle of the night?" she questioned skeptically.

He nodded, his mouth set in a grim line.

"Oh, Brad. You're getting ahead of yourself. We have no reason to think that."

"No? Then tell me why a common criminal breaks in without a trace, takes one seemingly valueless item, then leaves through locked doors and windows, again not leaving as much as a fingerprint."

Gillian's expression grew more reflective. "You're right. I'm going to have to call the bureau. If there's any chance our perp could be the one who broke in I wouldn't want to compromise any DNA evidence he could have left behind."

Brad knew she referred to the microscopic hair and skin traces that could be linked to the suspect. He noticed that she'd said she would call the bureau rather than CSU.

He saw why when they arrived. No explanations were needed as to why she'd dusted the desk and door frame before they arrived. Instead her people efficiently collected all possible evidence. They also took a strand of Brad's hair to eliminate him from their investigation.

When they left, Gillian turned to Brad with a wry smile. "So much for keeping the personal part of my life separate from the bureau."

He hadn't realized that was so important to her. "You did the right thing. If there's any chance that it could lead us to the kidnapper—"

"I know." Gillian pushed at her hair. Then she glanced around her living room.

"It stinks," Brad said for her. "Knowing someone was in here."

"Yeah."

He acknowledged the single word, aware how much it cost her. At the same time it reinforced the decision he'd made the moment he'd seen her gate standing open. "But you're not alone."

She glanced at him in question.

"I'll bunk on the couch. That way you can get some sleep."

"You're not the only cop here, Brad. And you need to sleep as well."

He stared at her. "Do you think I'd be able to sleep, thinking about the possibility of someone climbing in your window?"

Her eyes seemed to darken against her nearly translucent skin. "You wouldn't?"

His heart took the bump but kept on beating. "Of course not."

Tension was sudden, almost visible.

She glanced away. "I haven't had a babysitter since I was ten. Something you're ignoring."

He guessed it was she who wanted to ignore the awkward moment, along with reminders of the nights they had willingly spent together. "I know you won't call your family—you'd be afraid of worrying them. That leaves me. Which is more important? Your pride or staying safe to work on the case?"

Something indefinable flickered in her expression, before she nodded reluctantly. "I suppose you're right."

Brad felt about as wanted as last week's garbage. "Do you have an extra blanket?"

Stirred from her reflections, Gillian nodded. "Sure. I can even scrounge up a pillow. I'll see if I can find one that's not too soft."

He met her gaze. That was an intimate detail to remember.

From the way she shifted uncomfortably, he guessed she'd had the same thought. He was certain when she turned away, concentrating suddenly on gathering linen.

Making up the couch didn't take long. It was a near brainless chore. But the tug of shared history never left.

Brad watched Gillian's hands as they smoothed the cool sheets, remembering how she'd once strewn flower petals over the creamy linen. Candles had filled the room, but he'd needed only the moonlight gleaming upon her skin to see by.

She started to straighten up, her gaze caught in his. She swallowed. The quiet in the apartment seemed immense, and Brad couldn't summon one inconsequential bit of small talk.

Her voice when it finally emerged was unusually husky. "That'll be the bed, then."

Slowly he nodded.

She moistened her lips and didn't seem to know what to do with her hands. "I...uh, Brad. You really don't have to do this."

"We've been over that," he replied, his voice subdued, his thoughts riotous.

"So we have." She appeared to want to say more, or perhaps that was his own wishful thinking. She patted the pillow a final time. "Well, good night."

He nodded. It was too difficult to voice the words, to acknowledge that he and his wife would forever be separated by walls.

After she left, the minutes plodded by. He could hear the soft sounds of Gillian as she readied for bed. The crackle of one fabric, then the whispering slip of another.

Unwilling to feel like an eavesdropper on his own memories, Brad prowled through the living room looking for a distraction. But after a few minutes he realized it was unlikely he'd find anything. Every object in the room was Gillian's, and she was impossible to ignore.

Brad clicked on the television, went through the channels by rote, then turned it off again. He was too restless to even be lulled by a mindless sitcom, and the noise prevented him from hearing anything outside.

He switched off the lamp and stretched out on the couch. It was stupid, he knew, but he thought he could hear Gillian breathing. He could picture her in sleep, the way her face softened, revealing a vulnerability she normally kept well hidden.

Punching the pillow, he turned on his side, glancing around the dim room. As he watched, the thin line of light beneath Gillian's bedroom door disappeared. So she wasn't asleep yet.

Did she still hog the bedcovers? And wake up sprawled on the other side of the bed, her toes always wriggling free from the sheet?

Brad punched his pillow again, then stared into the darkness. Funny, it seemed a cop and an FBI agent would have had a better chance to stay together than the average couple.

Sighing, Brad rolled over, thinking of their time together.

It wasn't a bad way to spend the time, Brad acknowledged a few hours later. Because he wasn't going to sleep. His proximity to Gillian alone would have prevented that. But concern for her safety wouldn't allow it.

By then Brad had also memorized the contents of the living room, mentally developing a plan in case the intruder returned. Glancing at Gillian's bedroom door, he wondered if she'd managed to fall asleep. He hadn't heard anything for some time. He hoped weariness had overtaken her.

Deciding to warm up some coffee, he abandoned the couch. A small light remained burning above the kitchen window. Gillian said she usually left it on. They'd decided to make everything appear as usual. Brad glanced out the small window. Even as he did, he doubted the tight squeeze would be the first choice of an intruder. The rear of the property led down to a creek, making the unit vulnerable from three sides since it was on the end. The tall windows and French doors in both the living room and bedroom added to the vulnerability. What more could an intruder want?

Brad poured the coffee, put the mug into the microwave and programmed the machine. When it beeped, he retrieved his mug. Then he stood still for a moment, thinking he'd heard a faint sound. Silence.

But then there was another sound. Hot liquid splashed on his hand when he slammed the mug on the counter. Brad paid it no heed as he drew his gun. He crossed the living room in seconds, pulling open the bedroom door.

The room was empty. The French doors were open. Feeling his heart stop, Brad ran forward. Gillian stood at the gate, looking up and down the driveway.

He allowed a moment for the relief to register, then another movement caught his eye. It came from the top of the brick wall at the far end of the courtyard. Brad sped toward the wall and immediately heard the thud of someone dropping to the ground on the other side.

Cursing, he considered his options, not knowing if Gillian was armed. "Police! Freeze!" he shouted as he climbed the fence. But there was no one in sight when he reached the top of the wall. It was a perfect place to disappear. Tall trees and brush covered the land that sloped down to the creek.

He turned back and looked down. Gillian stood beneath him and he dropped down beside her. "You okay?"

"Yes."

He glanced at the gun she held. "I wasn't sure if you had that."

"Wouldn't be much point chasing him without it."

"Of course." When they were married it had always been hard to accept that she could defend herself. It didn't seem much easier now. "Did you see him?"

She shook her head. "I woke up, and the door was open. I reached for my gun and he ran."

"Why didn't you call for me?"

"I thought by the time you woke up..."
She glanced at his fully clothed state, taking
in the fact that he wore his shoes. Her expression changed, softened. "Didn't you
sleep at all?"

"I don't think that's our biggest concern.
He came back, Gillian. If he intended to re-
place the diary before it was noticed, he
knows now that can't happen."

"Or if he was simply a burglar, he might
have returned to finish the job."

"And steal what? Your stationery? You
don't believe that any more than I do."

"I've tried to keep an open mind, but he
is targeting me, isn't he?"

Brad couldn't keep the grimness from his
voice. "I'm afraid so. And now he knows
we're on to him."

Gillian glanced around the deserted courtyard. "This was always such a quiet place,
a safe haven."

Brad met her eyes. "But it isn't anymore,
Gillian. You won't be safe here again."

CHAPTER SEVEN

THE FOLLOWING MORNING Gillian combed through the reports yet again. She'd read and reread the scarce facts. And they continued to add up the same. All they really knew was that young Katie Johnson had disappeared exactly as Tamara Holland had. Volunteers continued searching the neighborhoods, fields and bayous near the missing children's homes. No ransom calls had been made and no one in the investigation believed there would be.

Lists of known pedophiles had been cross-checked against residents and employees of local businesses. Even offenders with records of simple assault had been investigated—still nothing. She and Brad, as well as the detectives, continued interviewing all neighbors and acquaintances.

It was as though Katie, like Tamara, had

just vanished. Gillian thought of Brad's sister, Amanda. The case was eerily similar in that aspect.

Shaking away the disturbing thoughts, Gillian wondered if there was an approach she hadn't considered. She had done everything by the book, used all the tools the bureau had at its disposal, yet she felt as though they were missing something. She rubbed at the spot between her eyebrows, trying to ease the aching in her head.

A light knock sounded on the glass of her office door, and Teri stuck her head in.

"Hey, what are you doing here?" Gillian asked in pleased surprise.

"I got tired of talking to your answering machine. And since you're probably surviving on coffee, I thought I might steal you away for a late lunch."

Gillian knew she couldn't spare that much time from the case. "We could order in."

"I knew you were working yourself to death."

Gillian hesitated.

"Then it must have to do with Brad. You want to talk about it?"

Gillian glanced at Teri, not surprised that her sister was so attuned. But she didn't want to worry Teri, so she edited the actual events, leaving out the intruder and Brad's presence on her couch. Brad had been right. It was the reason she hadn't asked Teri or her brothers to come to her aid. Not being cops, they wouldn't stop worrying once the case was concluded. "I hadn't really anticipated how it would feel spending so much time with him."

Teri murmured sympathetically. "Rough, huh?"

"Brings back a lot of memories."

"And emotions?" Teri guessed.

"Ah, the emotions," Gillian admitted ruefully. "They don't just disappear because a marriage ends and a piece of paper says they should."

Concern darkened Teri's face. "Second thoughts?"

"No. There's no future for Brad and me. That hasn't changed."

"What does he think?"

"We haven't discussed it, Teri."

"Why ever not?"

"Unlike you, not everyone is comfortable with shaking up things until something, or someone, falls out."

Teri shrugged. "It's more direct that way. If I'd have waited for David to propose I'd still be single."

"Be glad he appreciates that in you," Gillian said with a laugh. "Another man might have gone running."

"But I knew David wouldn't!"

"Lucky you."

"Yes, yes I am." Teri's voice softened with the acknowledgment.

Gillian suppressed a pang of envy. She didn't begrudge Teri her happiness. Still she wondered what it would be like to choose correctly the first time. Once she'd been nearly as sure.

She found herself wishing she could turn the clock back to those glorious first days with Brad. Could she have somehow changed the outcome? Changed his mind about having a family?

SEVERAL HOURS LATER, when Brad and Gillian were interviewing, he wondered why she was so quiet. She said there hadn't been any bad news concerning the case. But he couldn't help the feeling that something was wrong.

He glanced at his watch. "It's nearly ten. I need to run by my parents' house. Do you mind?"

She hesitated, thinking she needed to spend less time with him, not more. "That's fine."

He was beginning to worry about her. It wasn't like Gillian to be so subdued.

They reached the Mitchell home, and his parents were as welcoming as they had been the previous evening.

"You're sure I can't make sandwiches for you?" Elizabeth asked. "If I'd known you were coming I would have—"

"Gone to too much trouble, Mom. That's why I didn't call. I brought the router back so Dad can finish his project."

Thomas smiled. "I hope you didn't make a special trip. I haven't been in the workshop today."

Brad looked at him in surprise. "That's not like you."

"I know. But your mother talked me into going to counseling with her."

"Counseling?" Brad couldn't keep the shock from his voice. "Whatever possessed you to start counseling now? You're not having trouble, are you?"

Elizabeth laughed softly. "Not the kind you mean. But we need this therapy. Gillian talked me into it. I didn't think your father would agree, but he surprised me."

Thomas picked up Elizabeth's hand. "I know it's going to be good for us."

Brad couldn't believe his parents had agreed to counseling.

"I think so, too," Gillian added after an awkward moment of silence.

"Yes, of course," Brad managed to say.

Elizabeth smiled. "Your father and I talked for hours after you left. First thing this morning I called the psychologist Gillian suggested and he scheduled us based on her recommendation. Luckily, he had a cancellation and fit us in today."

"Did you like the psychologist?" Gillian questioned.

"Yes. He thinks we'll benefit from attending often."

"Counseling." Brad couldn't stop repeating the word.

Gillian's elbow connected with his side.

"Sounds great," Brad amended. "I hate to drop in and run, but we've had a pretty hectic day."

"We understand," Thomas replied.

"Of course," Elizabeth added. "But next time let me know you're coming and I'll cook."

Brad hugged his mother. "Sure, Mom."

"You come again, too, Gillian," Thomas told her as he opened the door.

Once they were outside, Brad could scarcely contain his surprise. "I can't believe you talked them into therapy!"

"Do you disapprove?"

"Of course not. It's just that we tried that when Amanda disappeared. It didn't do any good."

"As I said to your mother, it might be different this time. A lot of years have passed. Maybe it will help them."

"You have to feel a loss to understand

one, Gillian. I know your intentions are good, but I just hope you haven't raised their expectations for nothing. Someone was always offering us bits of hope, not knowing that each time the hope wasn't fulfilled it just made things worse."

"I see you haven't gotten over the misconception that you alone have suffered a loss."

Brad heard an unexpected edge to her voice. "Are you mad at me?"

"Why should I be mad at you?"

"Classic response of an angry woman. Okay, I'm sorry. For whatever it is. Truce?"

"I told you I'm not mad."

"Ouch. It's worse than I thought. Let's see. I didn't have onions on my hot dog at lunch. I don't kick dogs or pet rocks...."

"Pet rocks?" Surprise lifted the edges of her lips.

"Ah, so you *can* still smile." He was glad to see the change but still wondered what had upset her. "Why don't we grab a quick dinner?"

"I'm not all that hungry," she replied. "I had a late lunch with Teri."

"Then what if we swing by Baskin-Robbins? I haven't had a banana split in...well, too long."

"I don't know—"

"You aren't going to make me eat there by myself, are you? Nothing's sadder than a guy sitting alone at one of those tables for two. Take pity on me, Gilly Bean."

She glanced up, startled by his use of the pet name he'd given her.

He took advantage of her silence. "Great. You up for two or three scoops?"

Unable to choose just one flavor, she did agree to two scoops. Since they were the only ones in the ice cream parlor they took a table near the back.

"I wonder where all the kids are," Gillian mused, digging into her ice cream. The huge mound of whipped cream atop the sliced bananas started to slide.

Brad used his spoon to avert catastrophe, but ended up with most of the cream.

They were both laughing as he held the spoon up to her lips.

He wasn't sure when the laughter faded and her pupils dilated.

Her gaze went from his eyes to the spoon, then back again.

Slowly he retracted the spoon, all the while wishing he could lean across the table and kiss the sweet cream from her mouth, to whisper familiar words against them, as well.

She ducked her head, pretending great interest in the banana split. But neither of them seemed quite as enthusiastic.

Brad couldn't stand filling the silence with inane small talk. What had passed between them demanded more.

They were quiet as they left the store. When they reached the turn to her complex, Gillian glanced at him, looking puzzled. "I appreciate the ride, but we forgot to pick up my car."

"No sense driving back to the other side of town until morning."

"Excuse me?"

"Gillian, you really don't think I'm going to let you stay here alone after the break-in last night."

Something more than gratitude warmed her. "Oh?"

He reached into the back seat and withdrew a gym bag. "Besides, I like your couch."

She bit her lip. "If I call Teri or my parents and let them know what happened, they'll worry themselves sick."

"So would your brothers."

As they approached her place, Brad scanned the surrounding area. He noticed that Gillian did, too.

This time the gate was securely in place. It wasn't particularly reassuring.

The courtyard was quiet, seemingly undisturbed. As a precaution, Brad dropped his gym bag on the patio table so his hands could be free. Gillian put her purse there, as well.

He checked the need to be the one who opened the door, reminding himself that Gillian was also a cop, and it was her apartment.

She turned the handle on the French door, but it didn't turn. "It's still locked."

Brad admired her resilience. "Hmm."

She put the key in the lock. "Pessimist."

Brad watched intently as Gillian pushed open the door. The interior was quiet, still.

Gillian stepped in ahead of him. With his hand resting on his gun, Brad followed. A quick search told them they were alone.

"Do you see anything out of place?" he asked, inspecting the locks on the living room windows, seeing they were intact.

When Gillian didn't answer, he turned to her.

She stood next to the desk, staring at the surface.

"Gillian?" He went to her side. "What is it?"

"The diary," she said.

His gaze shot to the desk. Her diary was positioned at a slight angle beneath the banker's lamp.

They both knew not to touch it. Gillian couldn't seem to take her eyes from the leather journal.

"There's something else," Brad guessed.

She nodded. "The diary's in the exact position it was before it was taken. If I hadn't noticed that it was gone last night, I wouldn't have guessed it had been disturbed.''

Brad felt a chill that wasn't at all professional. As a cop he'd seen threats far, far worse than this. But this was directed at Gillian, and that unnerved him.

"I'll call the bureau.'' Gillian finally moved, heading toward the doors. "Why don't we wait in the courtyard?''

He agreed, not especially wanting to stay in the apartment. And neither of them wanted to further disturb any evidence before the crime unit arrived.

As they had the previous evening, the unit arrived quickly and worked with efficient precision.

When they were through, Brad noticed that Gillian looked exhausted. Having one's space violated did that.

The apartment seemed both empty and eerie to Brad. "Did they check to make sure the windows were locked?''

She nodded. "The guy's a real pro. He picked the exterior lock. I'll have to have a security system installed.''

"Good idea. But for now, you'd better pack a bag."

"What?"

"I could sack out on your couch, but we both need to get some sleep. And that's not going to happen here. We'll go to my apartment."

She shook her head. "No, no. Not necessary."

"Completely necessary. Unless you want to call someone in your family and stay with one of them."

"I can't do that. They'd never stop worrying, even once the case is over." She glanced around the living room. "I still haven't figured out how things got so out of control."

Brad hated to see her look defeated. "This guy's sinister. If he is our perp, he's stolen two children that we know of. Which means he'll stop at nothing, Gillian. We have to get you out of his line of fire."

"I know. But I hate it."

"You should. It keeps you alert."

She smiled weakly. "Now, that's a pep talk if ever I heard one."

"Do you need any help packing?"

"No. I'll grab my overnight bag."

"Gillian, better pack enough for a few days."

Her eyes were sober, but she nodded.

As she gathered her belongings, Brad roamed the living room, looking at all her personal touches. Uniquely framed pictures of her nieces and nephews perched on a golden Bombay chest. They were obvious indications of how much she loved her family.

Gillian stepped from the bedroom, looking a trifle forlorn as she clutched her suitcase. "I guess I'm ready."

Crossing the room, Brad reached for her bag. "Do you have everything you need?"

"I think so. It's weird. I feel like I'm escaping my own home."

"Then don't think so much," he replied, hating to see her so disturbed. "It's only temporary, Gillian. We'll catch this guy and you'll have your apartment back."

As they walked to the door, she turned and glanced back one more time. "I need to believe that."

Belief. That was something he had left behind so long ago he could scarcely remember the emotion. But he masked the thought, seeing that Gillian needed confirmation. And at least, for tonight, he was going to make sure she had everything she wanted.

GILLIAN FELT BRUISED as she entered Brad's apartment. It had been such a roller coaster of a day. And she couldn't imagine what had possessed her to stay at his place.

"Have a seat," Brad told her, carrying her suitcase off to what she guessed was the bedroom.

Glancing around, she saw that the apartment looked utilitarian. There was little trace of Brad.

"Wine?" Brad asked as he returned.

"That sounds good."

He flipped on the CD player, filling the room with soothing music, then retrieved a bottle of wine and two glasses.

She sipped the wine, glad for its gradual warming effect. Despite the heat of the summer evening, she'd been unable to shake the chill she'd felt since realizing both her home and private thoughts had been violated. And to know the intruder was toying with her simply compounded that feeling. "It's warming me up a bit."

Brad leaned forward. "Are you cold?"

"It's probably more mental than physical."

Yet he rose from the couch, adjusting the thermostat. "I'm gone so much I never think to check the temperature."

"Guess the whole thing creeped me out more than I want to admit."

"Because you're smart. We've both seen people who blind themselves to the truth, then suffer the consequences."

She fiddled with her glass. "Do you think he's been following the investigation?"

"Might fit. The efficiency of the abductions would correlate with a perp who wants to control every aspect of what's happening, perhaps following what's been released to the media."

"I think we should use my apartment as a trap for him."

Brad frowned. "We could try, but it won't do much good since he's on to us. He returned the diary because it put him in the power seat. I'm guessing he did it because he wants to see your reaction, enjoys being the hunter. But we could install hidden video cameras. If he breaks in again, we'll have him on tape.''

''The FBI has strict guidelines on any type of tapping, including video. It could blow a conviction.''

''I'm not FBI. And I'd rather find Katie Johnson and Tamara Holland alive even if it means a tougher time convicting.''

''Agreed.''

Gillian sipped her wine, then shivered despite her resolve.

''You're still cold.''

She tried to smile. ''Just my bones.'' Standing, she sought a way to shake away her disturbing thoughts. ''Do you mind if I wander?''

''Not at all. But I'm afraid there's not much to see.''

He was right. Even when they were married, he hadn't been one to display family photos. It was as though all those reminders were still too painful to face.

She sighed, again wishing that he'd been able to make peace with his past. Idly, she walked to the window. But she paused before judging the view. Carefully arranged on a slim table were half a dozen pieces of art glass.

Gillian turned to Brad in surprise. "This is the collection you mentioned."

"Yes."

She remembered the beautiful glass paperweight he'd given her father. Apparently the collection was something he treasured. Incredibly touched, she reached out to pick up the smallest piece. Although made of glass, it resembled tortoiseshell. The piece was unique, eye-catching, intriguing.

"This is exquisite. Which one did you get first?"

"The one you're holding."

So the piece had drawn him instantly, as well. "Any particular reason?"

When he didn't reply, she pulled her gaze from the paperweight to study his expression. "What?"

He shrugged. "It reminded me of you."

Stunned and touched, she felt the glass

warming in her hand. "Me?" she croaked in a voice unfamiliar to even her.

"Don't you see it?"

Battling a dozen conflicting emotions, she cleared her throat. "I'm not sure what you mean."

"The dark brown in the pattern is the same shade as your eyes." He reached out, touching the lighter golden color of the tortoiseshell design. "And this...this made me think of your personality, all sunshine and light." His fingers strayed over hers as he spoke.

Gillian wanted to give into the awareness that sprang to life at his touch, to bend to the warmth of his embrace. But that would be too temporal, the regret too lasting.

Still, she couldn't drag her gaze from his. There was so much history between them. Their marriage hadn't been long, but so much had been packed into that short time. Brad Mitchell was the love of her life, the man who consumed her heart, the man she'd nearly given up her dreams for.

And for that one reason she drew her hand back.

The disappointment on Brad's face mirrored what she was feeling, but he didn't try to recapture it.

Instead he retrieved the wine bottle. "Would you like some more wine?"

She nodded, uncertain how steady her voice would be.

He refilled her goblet, then brought it to her. "Will you be all right for a few minutes?"

Although she found her voice, it was strained. "Sure."

When he left she turned to stare at the beautiful glass. Gillian was amazed that a man who didn't have any other sentimental token on display had chosen to collect something so symbolic.

For the next several minutes, she sipped a little more wine, but it didn't relieve the coldness she felt.

When Brad returned, Gillian studied him uncertainly, wishing they could banish the awkwardness.

"Are you still cold?"

She rubbed her elbows. "A little."

"I think I have a cure. I drew a hot bath for you."

She blinked, hardly able to believe the words. "What?"

"I thought a hot bath might warm you up, help work out the kinks."

Incredibly touched, she gripped the stem of her goblet tightly. "That's so...so sweet."

His very male face took on a wry grimace. "Not the words we big, brave men live to hear."

Unexpectedly she smiled. "Darn sweet."

"Come on, you ungrateful wench, before it cools off."

She trailed behind him to the bedroom, seeing that her suitcase had been placed on the bed.

He pointed to an open door. "Bathroom's right there. Take all the time you want. I'll try to scrounge up something to eat."

"Maybe our mothers are right—perhaps we can't feed ourselves yet."

He pretended mock injury. "At least let me cook it before you insult my food."

She appreciated his attempt to dissipate some of the tension. "Deal."

Once he was gone, she retrieved her robe from the suitcase and stepped into the bathroom. Suddenly a hot bath sounded like the most inviting thing in the world. And the luxury of having someone else prepare it seemed wonderfully indulgent.

Stretching out in the tub, Gillian closed her eyes. The water was heavenly. She hadn't thought she could relax. But Brad was right. The tension in her muscles seeped away in the heat.

Gillian didn't know how many minutes had passed before she regretfully left the cooling water. Brad had provided fresh, thick towels. Feeling terribly spoiled, she slipped into her gown and robe.

As she entered the living room, Gillian felt unexpectedly shy. Immediately she was struck by the fire Brad had built while she was bathing. Considering it was a typically warm Houston night, it touched her that he would heat the apartment.

He glanced up, seeing her. "Do you feel better after your bath?"

"Incredibly better. You were right. It was just what I needed."

"That and a light supper."

"Can I help?"

"The kitchen's barely big enough for one person." He gestured to the bar stools. The counter had been set with two places. "Have a seat."

"You know, I could get used to this princess treatment."

His eyes darkened as their gazes connected.

Realizing it was a thoughtless, loaded comment, Gillian regretted it. "But one night of pampering should last me," she added, hoping to smooth over her gaffe. The look in his eyes told her she'd just made it worse.

"I don't have any tea or other hot drink, just coffee."

"That's okay." Wishing she could erase the words, Gillian settled herself on a stool. "I didn't think I was hungry, but that smells so good I feel my appetite making a comeback."

"Good." He reached for a plate, then slid

the food from the pan on to it. "I hope you still like jalapeño omelettes."

"Absolutely." She tasted the omelette. "It's delicious."

"Think our mothers would approve?"

Gillian dangled her bare feet over the cross bars of the stool. "Only if jalapeños count as vegetables."

He laughed, a deep sound in the otherwise quiet room. Then he filled his own plate and took the stool next to her.

They ate in companionable silence. Gillian hadn't thought she was hungry, but the familiar food was comfortingly warm and filling.

With her plate nearly empty, Gillian turned to Brad. "I know you don't want me to say it, but it's great of you to go to all this trouble. The fire, the bath, dinner. Thank you."

As he sat next to her, his gaze was even more intense. "You're welcome."

She fiddled with the remaining bits of egg, pushing the jalapeños into a line. "You're sure I'm not in the way?"

Looking genuinely surprised, he glanced over at her. "Of what?"

"Well, you know, your social life."

His brow wrinkled. "Ah. My *social* life. I don't have any pressing engagements."

The line of peppers became a circle. "I don't want to get in your way."

"Tell you what, Gilly Bean. When you're in the way, I'll let you know."

The pet name did more to warm her insides than the fire, bath and dinner combined. "Okay."

After they'd finished eating, Brad waved away her offer to help clean up, and Gillian strolled to the hearth. Glancing to one side she saw that the flames accentuated his brilliant glass collection. The tortoiseshell piece seemed to glow. Had Brad developed a sentimental streak? It hardly seemed possible, but then everything about the evening seemed improbable.

Turning around, she settled on the couch, tucking her feet under her. Leaning her head back, she closed her eyes. Gillian knew she shouldn't give in to the weakness, but it felt awfully good not to be on her own. The threat didn't seem as close with someone to share the worry.

Brad joined her and for a brief moment she was transported back in time. They'd spent many evenings in front of a warm fire, listening to music, simply enjoying each other. Their careers had meant long hours, but they'd always reserved time for themselves.

"Are you warm all the way through yet?" Brad asked quietly.

She considered gliding past the truth but couldn't bring herself to do so. "Yes. All the way." Inclining her head, she read the question in his eyes. But she didn't dare consider replying. Her gaze moved to his mouth, and the memory of how it felt against hers came to her.

Part of her wanted to forget the breakup, just seize the night and disregard the consequences. That had her stirring, then sliding away from him.

"Do you think you can sleep?" Brad asked, his voice gruff.

Nodding, Gillian rose.

Brad walked toward the bedroom. In a

few minutes he returned with sheets, blankets and a pillow.

She reached for a sheet. "Let me help."

One eyebrow lifted. It was an unconsciously seductive gesture that shot straight through her.

She focused her attention on the bed linen. Together they made up the couch. "This looks real comfy."

"I hope so." Brad picked up the pillow and bunched it up.

Gillian remembered the habit. Funny he should do it to her pillow.

"Do you need anything else?" Brad asked.

She glanced at the couch. "No, this looks great."

"It's not for you, Gillian. I'll take the couch. You can have the bedroom."

It was such a sweet gesture, she didn't know what to say.

Brad turned back the covers on the couch. "This way we'll both get a good night's sleep. You know I can fall asleep practically standing up and you're a light sleeper."

She glanced down at her toes, flushing at

the reminder of the intimacy they'd once shared.

Once in the bedroom she decided it wasn't such a terrible thing to be a princess. And, just for the moment, she could pretend that he was her prince.

CHAPTER EIGHT

YAWNING, GILLIAN STRETCHED, covering her eyes as the sunlight struck them. Turning over to bury her head beneath the pillow, she wondered why she'd forgotten to close the shutters in her bedroom.

Memory returned, fast and unrelenting. Swiftly she bounded upright and off the bed. A glance at the clock told her she was later than she wanted to be.

Pulling on her robe, she dashed out of the bedroom. The aroma of fresh coffee struck her as she entered the kitchen.

"Morning," Brad greeted her.

"Why didn't you wake me?"

"You needed the rest."

He'd always thought he'd known what was best for her. From inconsequential daily matters to the career she'd chosen. "Even so—"

"You forget you don't have your usual commute. We're only a few minutes from the precinct. I was just waiting for the coffee to finish brewing and then I was going to wake you up."

Slightly deflated, she pushed back at her rumpled hair. "Oh. I hadn't thought of that."

He handed her a mug of steaming coffee. "So, how did you sleep?"

"Really well." Much better than she'd expected. She'd felt warm and protected. And, despite all that had happened, sleep hadn't eluded her.

"Do you want some toast or something?"

"I'd better finish my coffee and get ready." Gillian took another sip of the aromatic brew. "You can take your shower first if you'd like." It was the routine they'd had when they were married.

"Okay. Won't take me long."

Gillian knew that but didn't comment. It was already seeming too familiar.

Her cell phone rang. Gillian was surprised to hear Vicki Campbell's voice. She was even more surprised and pleased that the detective had news. Promising to be in the office soon, she flipped the phone closed. "That was Vicki. There's been a sighting at the carnival. Someone suspicious watching young kids."

He was suddenly all business. "I'll make my shower quick so we can get on it."

Gillian thought about the possible lead as he disappeared into the bathroom. Realizing she needed paper to record some of the details, she chanced going into the bedroom to retrieve a pad from her suitcase.

She had the lid of the suitcase open when Brad emerged from the bathroom. Although he had a towel tied around his waist, she had an unobstructed view of the rest of his body. His shoulders were wide, his waist narrow and the remainder lean muscle—just the way she remembered him.

Throat dry, Gillian could imagine flinging herself against him. "S-sorry," she stuttered. "I needed to get my notebook. I thought you'd be in the shower."

"No damage down," he replied calmly.

Maybe not to him. "No, of course not. I'll just get my notepad." Suddenly she was all thumbs as she tried to pull it from her bag. It didn't help that he watched her clumsy efforts. As soon as the pad was free, Gillian raced from the bedroom.

Once back in the living room, she fanned her flushed face. Deciding she was being ridiculous, Gillian sat at the counter and forced herself to make notes about the assignment. She planned to have the detectives look into the route the carnival had taken and whether there had been any related crimes in those towns. They would also need to conduct background checks on the carnival employees. The suspect didn't seem to work there, but that didn't mean he hadn't found an accomplice. By the time Brad emerged from the bedroom, dressed for the day, she had regained her calm.

"Bathroom's all yours."

Gillian made her shower quick, dried her hair and dressed.

As they drove, Gillian filled him in on her plans.

Brad turned on the main arterial road leading to the station, merging into the already thick traffic. "What do we know about the suspect?"

"Nothing yet. And it may not pan out. People get skittish, turn in everyone but their grandmother when they're afraid a crime has gotten too close to home."

He glanced over at her and she realized he knew the drill as well as she did. "Sorry. My mind's just full. It's time we got a break. And yet I don't want to count on this one. This has been one of the hardest investigations I've ever been on. It's hard to believe two children can disappear and not one person see anything."

"You've done your best."

"I know. Procedures were flawless, but we've still come up empty."

"It's not a personal shortcoming, Gillian. You can't conjure up evidence if it doesn't exist."

"I feel like I'm letting Katie down, that she's counting on us for a miracle." The same miracle she wished for the Mitchells.

They had arrived at the precinct parking lot. Promising to reach him on his cell as soon as possible, Gillian left Brad and headed into the station.

The detectives began to filter in one at a time after Gillian was settled in her office. There was contagious excitement in the air as they learned of the possible break in the case.

According to the report, the suspect hadn't done anything other than watch. But one of the parents attending the carnival had become suspicious and alerted the police. Chances were the uniformed officers that responded scared off the suspect. However, the parent had been able to give a good description to the sketch artist. Flyers had already been distributed.

Seeing Vicki in the squad room, Gillian waved her inside. "Just who I was looking for. I'd like you to conduct the background checks on all carnival employees."

"Got it." She stepped toward the door, then turned back, looking pensive. "Gillian, you aren't planning to be a hero, are you?"

"What are you talking about?"

"Carnival surveillance. You didn't partner yourself with one of us, and Savino says he's assigned to stay here."

"Not counting my partner, there are five of us. No matter how you split that it comes out uneven."

"Are you going to take a uniform or someone from the bureau?" Vicki countered, looking worried.

"I'll have someone with me. I promise."

"Good. I've worked with hero types before and it's damn scary."

"Brad," Gillian guessed instantly.

"I don't know how you figured that out, but you're right. He's a great guy but it nearly gave me a stroke."

"Not my style," Gillian assured her.

After the detective left, Gillian remembered some of her earlier bureau days, ones in which she had still been with Brad. She'd been involved in a chilling case. Another agent's wife and child were killed out of revenge. Fearing as he had all along that Gillian, too, would be hurt, Brad demanded that she quit her job.

Knowing the scars Brad had, she'd tried to be patient and understanding, but she simply couldn't cope with his total inflexibility. Especially when he wouldn't consider giving up his own job. He had refused to see the connection. She doubted he would even now. Time to find their victims was evaporating. And she didn't want Brad to repeat the renegade behavior that had got him banned from the case.

Knowing he was waiting for her call, Gillian reluctantly picked up her phone, arranging to meet Brad at the carnival at three. She just hoped it wasn't a mistake.

BRAD HAD TAKEN CARE selecting his disguise. He knew he had to do more than simply blend in the crowd. He had to fool his fellow detectives, some of whom were also his friends. Even though most of them wouldn't want to report his activities, he couldn't put them in that position.

Brad rechecked his fake facial hair. He'd purchased good-quality theatrical props. While he wanted to remain unrecognized, he also didn't want to resemble a suspicious character. The well-trimmed beard and mustache looked neat while covering a good part of his face. He'd chosen a Houston Astros ball cap, knowing he wouldn't be the only person at the carnival wearing one. Sunglasses wouldn't be questioned in the bright sunlight. And his jeans were unremarkable, as was the baggy T-shirt that hid his true physique.

As he watched for Gillian, Brad realized he was looking forward to seeing her in something other than her professional clothes. He certainly hadn't minded the gown and robe she'd worn the previous evening. But he sensed that she had.

Gillian continued to be tense and jumpy around him. He hated that they were now polite strangers. How had it all gotten away from them? Should he have given in to her desire to have a baby? A shaft of familiar pain told him the answer. It wasn't in him to chance suffering another loss.

But then nothing about Gillian had fallen within his self-imposed rules. He had meant to protect his heart completely. He'd never intended to fall in love with her, with anyone. But Gillian was…well, Gillian.

His Gilly Bean. Instantly he could remember the laughter, the love, his certainty that she was the only woman he would ever care for. But she'd been unwilling to bend. He had tried to convince her they could be happy on their own, that they didn't need children to be content.

In the end all he could remember were her huge, sad eyes. They hadn't fought, because there hadn't been anything left to fight about.

Brad turned, spotting Gillian. Of course, she didn't need the disguise he did; still, he could have picked her out if she'd worn one.

Watching her walk closer he felt her grip on his heart, the one that had never lessened. It continued despite how much he'd tried to forget her.

Here she was again, on the front lines. And he no longer had the right to question her decision.

One of the nearby barkers extolled the benefits of the shooting gallery, his voice loud and inescapable. But Brad welcomed the intrusion, wishing it would drown out his thoughts.

Gillian was almost at his side. He was

about to reach out to catch her arm, when she stopped.

Brad glanced at his clothes. "My disguise that bad?"

Her eyes shifted away. "No. Just lots of practice. Have you spotted our suspect?"

"Not yet. I'm guessing he may be leery after the uniforms showed up last night."

She glanced down the midway. "I wonder if he'll show himself during the daytime either way."

"Since someone caught on to him at night, he may choose the afternoon hours. Kids will come here after they leave school for the day."

"Have you checked the layout?"

Brad shook his head. "Not yet. I've seen a few plainclothes officers."

"We need to cover all the grounds," Gillian replied. "I've seen photos, but I need to get a feel for the place."

They began to walk the sticky pavement.

"I used to love these carnivals when I was a kid," Brad admitted. That had been in the carefree days. After Amanda's disappearance his parents had been too fearful to allow him to attend anything that could possibly be dangerous. It had been a smothering time in his life.

"Me, too," Gillian agreed. "My parents would make Teri and my brothers bring me along. Naturally I did my best to torture them the entire time. They'd want to go through the tunnel of love with their dates, but it wasn't quite as romantic with me sitting smack between two of them."

Brad laughed at the image. "How'd I miss knowing you were the family tormentor?"

She shrugged. "I've always hated to brag."

He looked at the smile that reached her eyes and realized how much he'd missed these easy exchanges. She had an unparalleled gift for finding the most joy in every moment.

Gillian snagged his arm. "Look at that alley. Good place for a *watcher.*"

Brad felt an unexpected prickle at the base of his neck, the same one he'd felt when entering Gillian's apartment. It wasn't fear—that he recognized. Adrenaline always accompanied dangerous situations, but this was different. Immediately, he reached out, holding Gillian back when she would have plunged forward.

"What is it?"

"I'm not sure. Just a feeling."

She was immediately on guard, her voice low as she, too, scanned the area. "I don't see anything."

As they continued forward, Brad questioned whether or not his protective feelings for Gillian were affecting his instincts. He didn't see anything out of place, and although the cautionary prickle remained, he could see no physical reason for it.

"I don't see anyone."

Brad remained vigilant as they passed through the alley, looking back over his shoulder.

"What is it?" Gillian questioned. "Do you see something?"

"No."

"Still have a feeling, though?"

"My instincts may be skewed," he admitted.

"Any special reason why?"

He stared into her eyes and knew there was no answer. At least none he could give her. Instead he shrugged. "Nothing I can put into words."

"Hmm."

He wondered what was going on in that quick mind of hers. "What is it?"

"It's silly. Just thinking back on the days when a carnival was just a carnival—all childish fun, no worries or fears." She rubbed crossed arms. "Now it has a malevolent aura."

He looked at her in surprise. "That's what you feel?"

"It's nothing tangible. Just something about the place that doesn't seem right."

"Well, if a pedophile is being harbored here, that could account for it." Brad wondered as he spoke if that was the reason for his own uneasy feeling. He glanced back again toward the alley, but it remained unchanged.

They continued walking through the grounds. The carnival was still sparsely populated, which made it easy to check out. The fortune-teller watched them suspiciously as they passed.

"She probably knows exactly who comes and goes here," Gillian commented.

Brad glanced at the woman. "And it doesn't look like she wants to share."

"Maybe it's part of the act."

"Could be. Or she could know something."

"It's a relatively small group of employees," Gillian replied. "Seems logical that they'd all know one another pretty well."

"I'm guessing some of them must be drifters who don't stick with the carnival for long."

"Probably." They reached the Ferris wheel and Gillian looked upward. "We can get a bird's-eye view of the grounds from here, see if there are any other spots our guy might favor."

Liking the way her mind worked, he agreed they should ride the tall Ferris wheel.

As the steel cages rose in the air, they swung gently. Swaying in unison with her, Brad sneaked a look at Gillian. The breeze sent tendrils of hair across her cheeks. She caught her hair, peeling back a few strands that clung to her lips.

Brad couldn't stop looking at her mouth. Sitting close enough to simply lower his mouth to hers was more unsettling than he expected.

She didn't seem to notice his dilemma, instead she studied the grounds.

Brad told himself that he couldn't become distracted. This case was too important, the young victims were counting on him. He knew that as surely as he sat next to the woman he still loved.

And as surely as that would forever go unspoken.

CHAPTER NINE

AS AFTERNOON TURNED to evening, they still hadn't spotted the suspect. After school ended for the day, children had begun trickling in. And as the sun started to slowly sink, the crowd increased. Gillian wondered if Brad was right, if the suspect had been frightened away.

From a discreet distance, they watched one of the rides that carried passengers into a dark, cavelike interior. A quartet of children about the age of their victims crowded into one of the cars.

In silent understanding, she met Brad's gaze. *It would be so easy to snatch one of them, to disappear into the twilight.*

As she scanned the area, Brad suddenly draped an arm around her. The warmth of his touch penetrated her light cotton top, a delicious, well-remembered heat.

"Someone's watching us *watching*," he explained in a quiet tone.

"Oh." Gillian wished the word didn't sound so stilted, that she hadn't tensed up when she'd felt his touch. Turning her attention back to the job, Gillian looked across the midway. "Man in the gray T-shirt?"

"Yeah."

Suddenly the man stepped out, putting his hand on a young boy's shoulder.

Brad and Gillian moved forward the next instant.

A young woman pushing a stroller waved to the man. "We've been looking all over for you."

As they watched, the young family fell in step together, walking away.

Adrenaline mixed with relief, along with the realization they still hadn't spotted the perp. Gillian glanced at her watch. "It's time to meet with Turner and Fulton."

Brad nodded. "Can you find your way back to my apartment?"

"Yes." She glanced down the midway, watching couples, old and young, as they strolled through the attractions. "If we don't learn anything from the video cameras, you know what we'll have to do."

"Tell the team and the bureau," Brad replied.

"You don't sound surprised."

"Of course not. I don't want to be on the case so badly that I'd ignore your safety."

Gillian swallowed, realizing she was the one who was surprised.

Although it was dark, she could still see Brad's eyes. His gaze moved over her face, but then that impassive look he wore so well filled his expression.

Gillian pushed the emotion from her voice. "Did I tell you I'm considering a bigger sweep of the carnival area—coordinating it with the bureau?"

"This morning," he replied.

Gillian slowed her too eager words, realizing she was talking to cover her nervous reaction. She needed some distance. "After I meet with Turner and Fulton I'll swing by the station."

"Can't it wait until morning?"

But she wasn't in the mood to negotiate. "Goes with the job."

Brad nodded.

She knew he couldn't say more—that he couldn't risk being seen by the detectives. So she fled.

AND GILLIAN DIDN'T STOP running until she reached the relative safety of the station. Her meeting with Turner and Fulton hadn't taken long, for which she was grateful, wanting to be gone from the carnival and from Brad's proximity.

Now, enclosed in her borrowed office, Gillian pondered the day, the case, the increasing time she was spending with Brad.

Vicki stuck her head in. "You hibernating?"

"You're a fresh breath of air. Come in."

"Any special reason you need fresh air?"

"You're entirely too observant, Vicki."

"Occupational hazard. The case getting to you? Or is it something more personal?"

Gillian would like nothing better than to pour out her feelings to a detached third party and secure an honest opinion. But that wasn't possible. "Guess it's just the world in general."

"Well, if that's all…" Vicki studied Gillian as she sank into the chair across from the desk. "Jeez, you do look like you're carrying the weight of the world. You want to tell me about it?"

"Yes. But I can't."

"Isn't this a fun new game?"

Unexpectedly, Gillian found her smile returning.

"That's better," Vicki declared. "I was wondering if I should call the paramedics."

"It's not quite that grim."

Vicki's partner, Shawn Spiers, tapped on the door of the office and stepped inside. He didn't waste time with greetings. "There may be a pattern."

Gillian listened to Shawn's report, gripped by the feeling that they were finally on to something.

"Two and a half months ago, while the carnival was in Tyler," Shawn continued to explain, "a ten-year-old girl disappeared."

"Was she ever found?"

Shawn shook his head. "They weren't sure at first if she was a runaway, but no clothes or favorite possessions were gone. Like Tamara Holland and Katie Johnson, she disappeared in the middle of the night."

Gillian frowned. "And no witnesses?"

"Not one. It's a quiet neighborhood."

Like their victims.

Shawn nodded. "There are a lots of similarities. The Tyler police searched the area, canvassed the neighborhood, but they didn't turn up anything."

"Were the parents ever suspects?"

"No. The mother was home with the other children. The father was at work on the night shift with fifty other people, never out of their sight." Shawn paused. "On a hunch, I checked to see if she was a Girl Scout."

"And?"

"She was an active member. It's a common link."

Gillian considered this. "But the carnival isn't. Interview Deerling again tomorrow."

"Right," Shawn agreed.

"Vicki, I need the carnival's employee profiles."

The detective stood. "Be right back with them."

Shawn handed Gillian the Tyler girl's report. "Do you want me to keep researching other towns the carnival performed in?"

"Yes. I hope there's not a bloody trail across the state, but if there is, it's time we found out."

Shawn met her gaze. "How are we going to cover this?"

"I'll go to Tyler tomorrow. You and Vicki talk to the Johnsons again tomorrow, as well. Primary carnival surveillance will go to Fulton and Turner, with backup to split their shift. Agent Savino will coordinate the task force in Houston."

Now all Gillian had to do was tell Brad. And decide whether he would take this next step with her. Or whether it was time to go it alone.

BRAD WATCHED OUT HIS living room window, the bright city lights a constantly changing panorama, one he didn't really see. His mind was on the phone conversation he'd just had with his mother. He couldn't remember when she'd sounded so upbeat. He was surprised by her new attitude, but even more surprised by her request. She wanted him to consider counselling, as well. Reluctantly he wondered if she could be right.

He heard a tentative knock on the door, one that was nearly as soft as the music he'd selected. Before he opened the door, Brad knew it was Gillian. It wasn't like her to be tentative. But something had changed in her that afternoon. He didn't know why, but the shift had been visible. At least to him.

And her face still reflected that change.

"Come on in."

"I have news," she announced, barely inside.

"Good news?"

"We may have a connection."

Brad put aside thoughts of his personal life. He was amazed that the change wasn't more welcome. Normally, work was his prime consideration, especially this kind of case. Taking Gillian's briefcase from her, Brad placed it on the end table, listening as she filled him in.

When she finished, she looked at him expectantly. "I think it's the break we've been hoping for."

"Sounds like it."

Her expression grew puzzled. "You don't sound very pleased."

Brad forced his thoughts to settle. "It's a mixed bag. I'm glad we have a connection, but I can't be pleased we have another victim. Are you going to Tyler?"

She hesitated. "Yes."

He gestured to the bar stools. "You look beat. Wine?"

"Just a small glass."

He poured the wine, then passed her a glass.

She sipped the satisfying merlot. "I didn't realize how tired I was."

He pulled take-out Chinese food from the oven. Handing her a carton and chopsticks, he took the stool next to her.

She inhaled the spicy scent. "It smells delicious."

They ate the warm food, the toll of non-stop work and lousy eating habits having caught up with them.

When Gillian reached the bottom of the carton, she fiddled with the chopsticks. "You don't have to feed me, you know."

"I know."

She pushed at the last bite of chicken. "And you don't have to protect me."

"So you keep telling me."

She laid her chopsticks down. "Okay, what's with you?"

"Can't you just accept that I'm being agreeable?"

"Why?"

He sighed. There was so much between them. And no time to resolve any of it.

"I'm sorry," she added quickly. "That wasn't very gracious. I appreciate your concern, but I've become accustomed to watching out for myself."

"Point taken. Fortune cookie?"

Distracted, she accepted the cookie.

Cracking open his own, he expected the usual cryptic message. Still, the words surprised him. "Love will be yours with the light."

Meeting Gillian's eyes, he tucked the message into his pocket. And, taking a huge leap, allowed himself to hope.

CHAPTER TEN

GILLIAN WASN'T SURE HOW Brad had managed it, but he was beside her as they drove into the East Texas town of Tyler. Deciding to pass off her acquiescence as temporary fatigue, she resolved to get back in control.

However, it was difficult to maintain her annoyance as they rode through the deep green landscape. The farther they traveled from Houston, the more she felt her tension retreat.

Entering Tyler, the rose capital of Texas and—in its citizens' opinion—that of the country, Gillian sighed. The sweetness of blooming roses was so at odds with their mission.

They easily found the police station. The locals were eager to share their information, to enlist any help in finding the young victim. But the Tyler police weren't optimistic about still finding the girl alive. She had been gone for nearly three months.

After studying the files, Gillian and Brad drove to the girl's neighborhood, which was calm, quiet and pretty.

Brad parked across from the victim's house. "Looks like an ideal place to raise children."

"I wonder how many of the parents are scared to death now," Gillian questioned aloud.

"All of them would be my guess."

"I don't understand why your captain barred you from the case." Gillian blurted out words she'd been thinking but hadn't meant to say.

"What?"

"You seem to have such a good handle on all the aspects of a disappearance. And you'd work all day, every day given the chance. You also seem completely in control of yourself. I know you said you blew a kidnapping case. But what exactly happened?"

He turned away, hesitating. "I hadn't been at the precinct long. A particularly nasty case came up—abduction of young boys who were raped and beaten, some found more dead than alive. The last one died on the way to the hospital. We collared the perp and I lost it.''

Gillian could picture his anger. And while she didn't blame him, she could also understand his captain's point of view. ''And Maroney hasn't given you a second chance?''

''Internal Affairs wrote me up for my treatment of the bastard—violation of his civil rights. Top brass wasn't happy.''

''Which puts your captain on the line if he lets you handle another one and you go ballistic.''

''Yep.''

Gillian knew she'd taken a chance in allowing him to work on the case unofficially. But the sinking pit in her stomach told her it could mean the end of both their careers if anything went wrong. She reached for the door handle. ''You ready?''

''As much as I ever will be.''

Gillian knew Brad dreaded interviewing the victim's parents. They would be touching an unhealed wound, refreshing their pain.

The discussion didn't last long. The parents, clearly agonized, were desperately eager to share what little information they had. But, like Tamara's and Katie's parents, they didn't know anything other than the fact their child had disappeared. Time hadn't brought any more memories to the surface that could provide a lead.

Gillian and Brad glanced at each other before climbing in the car. Their exchange was silent, their agreement complete. Talking to victims' families was the worst part of the job.

They drove around the neighborhood. It was comparable in many aspects to both Tamara Holland's and Katie Johnson's. But there was no trail to follow.

While still in Houston, Gillian had called to have other agents interview neighbors and run background checks. Until they learned more, she couldn't be certain the crimes had a correlation.

Her cell phone rang. Gillian listened, jotted down a few notes and turned to Brad with an unhappy expression. ''There was another disappearance farther east in Callville, another town the carnival performed in.''

Brad glanced at his watch. ''That's not too far. We probably have just enough time to make it there before dark.''

Gillian considered the wisdom of traveling on with Brad. However, she had prepared herself that it could be an overnight mission. Deciding business was more important than her personal concerns, she phoned the agent who would be coordinating the interviews in Tyler. Assured that he could handle everything that entailed, she decided to go with her gut feeling and drive on.

But their calculations were off. It was well past dark when they arrived in Callville. They had encountered an unexpected detour. Construction took them on a bumpy two-lane farm road most of the way.

''Are you hungry?'' Brad asked when they finally reached town.

''I'm guessing that's your way of saying we should wait to contact the locals.''

''Put yourself in their place. The FBI and HPD roll in unannounced when the chief's no doubt gone home for dinner. We can phone them, get something to eat and then look at the files.''

"I suppose you're right," Gillian conceded. "And I'm starving.''

Driving down the sparse main street, they figured the local diner would be the best choice.

Brad parked the car, glad to stretch his legs after the hours of driving. Gillian phoned the local sheriff's office from the parking lot, not wanting to attract attention from the patrons. Then she checked in with the task force in Houston.

Once inside, Brad was relieved to see the place looked clean and hospitable. It took him only moments to decide he wanted the chicken-fried steak. He enjoyed watching Gillian as she perused the menu. He'd always liked the fact that she was no snob. Some women would have considered the rural diner and its plain menu beneath them. Not Gillian.

"Um," she said aloud. "I shouldn't, but I'm having the chicken-fried steak with extra gravy.''

Brad glanced at a display of homemade desserts. "Me, too. And pie."

The food was hot and delicious. Hungry and tired, they ate with little conversation.

Gillian finished her mashed potatoes and smiled in a teasing way he remembered well. "Our mothers would be pleased we're having vegetables."

Brad knew his mother would be pleased that he was spending so much time with Gillian. She had always believed they would find their way back together. While that might be a far-fetched idea, this time had been a gift.

"Have you talked to my mother lately?"

Gillian shook her head. "Is something up?"

"You could say that. She's even more certain the counseling is helping her."

Gillian's smile was gentle. "I couldn't be happier."

"She thinks I should go to counseling, too."

Fiddling with the salt shaker, Gillian hesitated. "What do you think about that?"

"It never did any good before."

Wiping her hands carefully on the paper napkin, Gillian didn't meet his gaze. "And now?"

Brad considered the possibilities that had been plaguing him. "I don't know."

She drew patterns in the condensation that coated her glass. "What if it could help?"

He pushed back in the booth. "Sounds like you think I need it."

"Brad, I want you to be happy."

"Do you, Gillian?"

"Of course I do. We're divorced, not enemies."

"Then you should know I did take a risk."

Her lips trembled suddenly. "This isn't the time. With the case—"

He relented, realizing she was right. "It's a strange path we've taken, isn't it, Gilly?"

Her throat worked, and he watched the fragile trembling with an ache that had never completely left him since they'd split up.

But she didn't speak. And when she looked at him with her huge eyes, he wanted somehow to make it better, to tell her what she'd wanted to hear, what he'd never been able to commit to.

Instead he forced his expression to clear. "You still want to meet with the sheriff's office tonight?"

She cleared her throat. "Yes. I'd like to study the files."

Although he would work on the case twenty-four hours a day—as Gillian had said in the car—Brad wondered if their perspective was becoming affected by the long hours.

However, once at the sheriff's office, the search took an unexpected turn. The deputy had pulled the files on the disappearance of Holly Brewster. The girl turned out to be seventeen years old. The case could be connected, but at that age the victim could well be a runaway. Details on interviews with family and friends were sketchy, confirming that the sheriff's office shared that opinion. With the deputy's permission, they took copies of the meager files.

Once outside, Brad glanced at Gillian. "There's not much to go on."

"Agreed. The connection seems pretty

tenuous. Why don't we give ourselves a break? Get some sleep.''

There was only one motel in the small town. Located on the main drag, its fifties-style neon sign declared it had soft beds and hot coffee.

A bittersweet nostalgia gripped Brad as they completed separate registration cards.

The man handed them each a key. ''I'll send my wife over to check out the rooms. Should be ready in about thirty minutes.''

''So much for relaxing,'' Gillian muttered.

''Why don't we take a walk until the rooms are ready?'' Brad suggested. ''It's a tolerable evening.''

She smiled. ''Tolerable? I guess that still says it all.''

Away from the distraction of big-city lights, the stars seemed nearly within reaching distance. The silvered moonlight scuttled over tall East Texas pines and dewy grass.

''It's quiet,'' Gillian commented. ''At home I don't mind the traffic and city noise, but…''

Brad remembered their dream to move to

the outskirts of the city, to design a home to take advantage of the peaceful setting. "Yeah. I know."

The silence lingered between them, but whatever was left unsaid was understood by both of them.

The sound of their footsteps crunching on the gravel was louder than the hum of moths and busy mosquitoes as they dove toward the lights lining the motel's porch.

"The smell of honeysuckle is really strong," Gillian said finally.

Brad knew she was trying to break the strain, but he didn't feel like small talk, preferring to walk, instead. "Yeah."

However, Main Street wasn't very long.

"We're about to run out of pavement," Gillian remarked, turning beneath the single street lamp.

The light shone on her in such a way that Brad caught his breath. What was it about this woman that moved him as no one else ever had? He wished he could simply give in to what she wanted so that he could make her his again.

Instead he offered the best smile he could muster. "Can I buy you a Coke?"

She glanced around the deserted looking street, but her lips edged upward. "Where?"

He pointed to a small machine in front of an ancient gas station.

"You big spender," she teased.

In unison, they approached the vintage vending machine and Brad dug into his pocket for coins.

"The Cokes are in little bottles!" she squealed.

"And you think I don't know how to impress the ladies," he replied mildly, putting his change in the slot.

The quarters clunked their way down the passage and the bottles plopped into the chute with a pleasing sound.

"This is amazing," Gillian continued. "It's like a town out of time."

He smiled at her whimsy. He had always liked the fact that she could shed her professional demeanor and have fun.

She glanced up at him. "What?"

Brad shook his head. "Nothing." He

looked up at the full, dark sky. "Just thinking what a pretty night it is."

"These little towns seem too peaceful to contain the crime we're encountering."

"Appearances can be deceiving."

She toed the tip of her shoe into the loose gravel. "Uh-huh."

It wasn't to be a night of more revelations, Brad realized. Gillian was drawing in—her form of self-protection. He decided not to push her. "Maybe this town is just as it appears. And maybe it was too small for a seventeen year old. This girl could have run away. She might be safe somewhere."

"We'll deal with it, no matter what it turns out to be."

Brad reminded himself that his former wife was no wilting flower needing to be propped up. Funny, he'd never realized that fact with such clarity.

They walked back down the street, aware of the increasing breeze, the scents of summer flowers and newly mowed grass, aware of what they weren't speaking about. The minutes passed and without speaking they returned to the motel to find the rooms were ready.

Gillian's room was at the end of the main sidewalk; Brad's next door, but around the corner. The wind was picking up quickly, nearly snatching the files from Brad's hands.

Stepping inside, Gillian kept her fingers crossed, hoping that the place was clean. And was gratified to catch a whiff of lemon oil and disinfectant. Although tidy, the rooms were small, not surprising considering the era of the motel. That meant a solitary hard wooden chair, end table and a bed that looked no wider than a matchbook. She reached for the knob on one of the two doors, expecting to find a closet. But the door was locked.

"It's a connecting door." Brad's muffled voice traveled through the wall. "I've unlocked my side if you need anything."

No. That wasn't going to happen. "Thank you."

Picking up the small bag she always carried when she was going out of town on a case, Gillian slipped into the bathroom. Once in the shower, she stood under the stream of strong, hot water, glad to wash away the remainder of the day.

Out of the shower and beginning to towel off, she heard the deepening howl of the wind, realizing a storm must be approaching. Glad to be securely inside, she donned shortie pajamas, then smoothed lotion over her hands and legs.

Although it wasn't late, she was tired. And the small bed was suddenly very appealing. Ingrained habit kicked in and she placed her gun on the bedside table.

Stretching out, she closed her eyes, wondering if her unresolved thoughts would allow her to sleep. Physical exhaustion overcame emotional distress, and she fell asleep within minutes.

Brad held the hand of a little girl. Gillian held the child's other hand as they lifted her to skip over a curb. Brad laughed as the child—their child—giggled with delight. Gillian saw her own joy as well. They were the perfect family—husband, wife and child.

As she watched, a dark, shadowed man approached, threatening them all. Gillian tried to fight back but was helpless. Brad shielded her, along with the child. But she should have been able to help.

In her sleep, Gillian vainly struggled. Eventually spent, she gave in to deeper sleep where the dream didn't torment her.

Hours passed as her mind restored itself.

And then the noise of glass shattering filled the room.

Jerking upward, Gillian couldn't tell at first if the noise was real or an extension of her earlier dream.

Wind and rain gusted toward her, slapping her unprotected face and arms. At the same time, Gillian heard pounding on the connecting door.

Shaking off the temporary paralysis of surprise, she ran to the connecting door, unlocking it.

Brad pushed past her, his gun in hand as he quickly surveyed the room. Seeing the broken window, he flung open the door and darted outside to look around the parking lot.

Gillian grabbed her gun and followed.

Brad turned back before she reached him, shutting the door against the fierce weather.

"I can't see anyone." Still he turned the lock.

"So it's just the storm?"

"As far as I can tell." He glanced at the ruined window. "We can call the manager from my room."

He didn't have to coax her. The storm had turned the night unseasonably cold. And a different sort of shiver reminded her that it wasn't only the weather that chilled her.

Once in his room, Brad pulled his jacket from the chair, draping it over her shoulders.

"Thanks." She glanced at him, clad only in jeans. "You must be freezing."

"I'm okay." He reached for the phone, listening for a few moments, then replaced the receiver. "Phone's out. I'll go to the office, tell the manager about the window."

She started to pull the jacket from her shoulders.

"Keep it." He donned his shirt, buttoning it as he crossed to the connecting door and locked it. "I'll use my key when I come back."

The room seemed unbelievably empty once he was gone. Walking over to the window, she watched as he ducked into the office. He wasn't there long before he emerged, holding two foam cups.

She pulled back from the window, grabbing towels from the bathroom. The key turned in the lock.

Although Brad was drenched, he held out one of the cups. "Coffee?"

She accepted it, handing him the towels. "Thanks."

He put down his own cup, then pulled off his soggy shirt, toweling his hair and upper body. "Manager says he'll nail some boards over the window, but he isn't sure it will keep out all the rain."

"Oh."

"In case it wasn't the weather, it would be a good idea to stay together."

Gillian didn't relish the thought of returning to her waterlogged room. Especially alone.

Brad reached for his coffee. "Doesn't taste half bad."

She dragged her gaze from his body. "That's high praise for you."

He met her eyes and she knew he didn't want to discuss the merits of the coffee.

Unwilling to discuss anything else, she took refuge in a swallow of coffee. Not expecting it to be so hot, she choked on the scalding liquid.

He was next to her in a flash. "Jeez, Gillian, you know you can't drink stuff as hot as I like." He took the cup from her and then held her arm high in the air to open her air passages.

Still sputtering, she pushed her hair from her eyes. "You're right."

A touch of exasperated humor touched his eyes. "At least about something."

She smiled tentatively, hoping they could broker some sort of truce. "About a lot of things." To hide her nervousness about that admission, she reached for the files the sheriff's office had supplied.

"You're going to work *now?*"

Gillian knew she had to distract herself. "I know it's late, but I'm too wired to sleep. I'll be quiet."

He sighed. "That's not a concern. I won't

sleep.'' Brad retreated into the bathroom, returning with a glass of water for her.

The cool water eased her scalding mouth. ''Thanks.''

He pointed to the file she held. ''So, what's ticking in your head?''

She opened a folder. ''I'm wondering why no more effort was put into finding the vic.''

''Deputy said they thought she was a runaway,'' he reminded her.

''I know, but still...'' Gillian drew her eyebrows together. ''This is such a small town. You'd think everyone would pull together to find a missing teenager. Unless there's something more...''

''Deep, dark secrets?''

She shrugged. ''I don't know if it's sinister. But I have a feeling—nothing I can put into words. But it seems like something's missing here.''

Brad picked up a stack of papers, forcing himself to study the words instead of Gillian. Some of them actually penetrated. ''Looks like the stepfather didn't seem very concerned.''

"I noticed that. And the mother's account is noticeably brief."

"Maybe he does the talking for both of them." Brad scanned the second page. "Do you want to start with them in the morning?"

"Yes. And if we catch a break maybe we can talk to the mother alone." Her voice softened. "I can't imagine a mother not caring what happens to her child. It seems so unnatural."

Why was it every conversation they had seemed to come back to the sore point between them?

Gillian sifted through the remaining pages. "And why didn't they interview her friends? At that age, they're bound to know more than the parents." She glanced up at him. "Don't you think?"

"Actually, I'm not sure I have enough perspective to answer that. Amanda disappeared while I was in high school. My parents were so afraid something would happen to me that they didn't give me as much freedom as my friends. So I didn't get to hang out with the other kids that much."

Gillian's eyes clouded. "That's a heavy burden for a teenager. Indeed, for all of you."

Brad knew what she was leaving unsaid. That he hadn't recovered from that time. But he had moved on as much as he could. He wasn't sure there wasn't any chance of his healing more. Surely if there was he would have by now.

Gillian passed a hand across her forehead. "I'm sorry. I keep picking away at you. I don't mean to. I really only want you to be happy."

It was the second time in about as many hours that she'd expressed the same feeling. This time he didn't feel like questioning her sincerity. "Maybe happy endings aren't in the cards for everyone."

She met his gaze, her eyes liquid with regret and pain. Her voice was raw with both. "I guess not."

He felt the words bubbling inside him that needed to be spoken, that should have been spoken long before now. "I'm sorry about that, Gilly."

Her lips trembled. "Yeah. Me, too."

He wasn't completely sure who took the first step. But suddenly his arms were around her, her shuddering body filling his hands, her bereft expression filling his heart.

Gillian breathed in the wonderful smell of him, savoring the feel of his lean, muscled body against hers. Closing her eyes against the waves of sensation and memories that crashed over her, she wanted nothing more than to continue melting in his arms.

His mouth found hers. Hot, impatient, greedy. Knowing she should pull back but unable to, Gillian reveled in the perfect fit of their lips, an alignment of body and heart.

Heart! Nagging shreds of reason thrust past her rebellion. Her heart couldn't take the pain of losing Brad again, of knowing that no matter how much they loved each other, they weren't destined to be together.

Despite the shiver that went through her, she let herself feast on him, desire chipping away at her resolve. And Gillian wondered if that, too, had impossibly taken flight.

CHAPTER ELEVEN

BRAD'S LARGE HAND CUPPED her breast, and Gillian felt the remainder of her breath whoosh out. How she'd missed his touch, dreamed of it, longed for it.

Heat was instant, going from zero to raging in the span of a single second.

She felt the trembling, the quaking, the singular joy that struck body and soul when she was with him. Her fingers pushed into his thick hair, grasping for a steady hold in the suddenly rocking world. His muscles were as tight as she remembered, his skin supple over that strength. She'd always loved that dichotomy, the pure maleness of him.

Panting, she pulled away, trying to hide how much she wanted him.

"Gillian," he murmured, his voice gruff.

"This is…" She tried to stem her fugitive

pulse, which gave her the feeling that she had just run miles, or needed to. "This is madness. We both know it."

His strong hands moved over her shoulders, caressing, invoking. "Ah..."

There were thousands of things that needed to be said, but not one would be uttered.

Gillian met Brad's eyes, seeing the desire, the regret. She guessed her own expression was the same. Straining toward him, she wondered why Brad and only Brad could elicit such a response from her.

But love wasn't about caution or reason, she acknowledged weakly before moving back into his arms.

Gillian felt the silky fabric of her pajamas slide away, and she became impatient to remove the barrier of his clothing as well. Her hands were greedy, tugging at the button and zipper of his jeans. He aided her efforts, pulling free of the restricting fabric.

Long-denied flesh sought sinewy muscles and tender skin. Hard against soft. Male against female. Husband joined with wife.

Thoughts surfaced, fled and melded as

their hands spoke the words they couldn't say. Gillian nibbled a path of kisses over Brad's abdomen, her own desire quickening as he sucked in his breath, then shuddered beneath her hands.

He shifted, bringing his body over hers, using his lips to nip the tender skin of her throat, then tease her breasts with kisses that lengthened until she moaned beneath his caresses.

His hands and mouth wove a familiar path over her waist, traveling downward as she trembled under his knowing touch, until her skin became a blanket of sensation.

She gasped as they were joined together, needing this feel of him, savoring it, holding on to each moment. Briefly closing her eyes, Gillian welcomed his possession of her.

Gripping his shoulders tightly, she pulled as close to him as physically possible. Sensing her need, Brad stroked her hair, then gently captured her lips.

In that instant her heart stuttered.

And, for just this one moment, she pretended that all was right.

BRAD FELT THE DEAD WEIGHT on his arm and wondered why the limb had gone to sleep. As he was poised to turn, a warm breath whispered across his cheek.

Memory slammed into him, a fist nearly as powerful as the desire for the woman sleeping next to him.

Judging by the gray cast to the room, it was still early. However, there was enough light to illuminate Gillian's face. Knowing what they shared was probably temporary, and that he might not have another opportunity to study Gillian in her sleep, Brad savored each moment.

Her flawless skin was rosy, and he held his hand in check with an effort. He contented himself with counting the freckles that were sprinkled over the bridge of her nose. She'd despaired of them, but he thought the small imperfections added to her allure.

His gaze went to her lips, slightly parted as though in expectation. Curled up on her side, she stirred him yet again.

Her hair would still be soft, he knew. Although he'd never told Gillian, he'd found it comforting to stroke her hair, to luxuriate in the feeling of having her close, knowing she was safe. There had been too much left unsaid, he realized.

He swallowed against the feelings, knowing she wouldn't change her mind, despite what they'd shared. She'd been his once, but she was too smart to take another chance with him. He admired her control. But he had to admit to himself that he wanted her as much today as the first time. And he didn't know if he could bury that desire again.

He longed to look deep into her velvety eyes, but in the light of day, they might hold wariness, shutting him out again. So he contented himself with watching the even rise of her breathing, the flush of her skin, the invitation in her lips.

When she turned in her sleep, releasing his arm, he studied her for a few last minutes. Then, with regret, he got up. Although he could have spent the entire morning watching her, he guessed she would be uncomfortable when she woke. And he couldn't face her regret.

Quietly he stole into the bathroom, trying to shower away his conflicting feelings, eventually turning the water to cold. It didn't help, so once shaved and dressed, he decided to walk off some of his tension. As he left the room, he looked at her, committing the vision to memory before he stepped outside.

The storm that had swept in with such ferocity had departed, leaving only quiet. Leaves and downed branches littered yards, but the street was clear.

Callville was sleepily awakening as well. A young man yawned as he unlocked the front door of the gas station. And from the café, the strong, invigorating smell of brewing coffee saturated the air.

Brad thought about Gillian's intuition—that something about this girl's disappearance was amiss. Gillian was a damn fine agent and he trusted her instincts.

However, studying the small town, he couldn't see any obvious aberrations. Callville was a picture-postcard version of rural America. If there were secrets behind the gingham-checked curtains, they were hidden well.

Brad strolled over to the café, taking the opportunity to study the semirolled-up main street. Once in the diner, he slid into a Naugahyde-upholstered booth and ordered coffee. The thick stoneware mug warmed his hands but didn't reach the cold pit in his stomach. The pit was caused by fear. Fear that he and Gillian were destined to be apart. Knowing he needed to hide that from her, Brad drank a second cup, hoping it would quell the feeling.

Watching the customers straggle in, Brad didn't see anyone suspicious. Just the regular assortment of everyday people. He figured most of them knew one another, especially since their greetings consisted mostly of grunts and nods.

Accepting another refill, Brad stalled as long as possible. But he'd seen enough surreptitious glances to know he'd begun to attract attention. His and Gillian's presence would no doubt travel the grapevine soon, but no sense giving the locals a head start.

When he returned to the motel room, he knocked on the door.

''Come in,'' Gillian called out.

Brad turned the knob cautiously. He wasn't sure he could handle another glimpse of Gillian's shapely legs.

Brad didn't know whether it was relief or disappointment he felt when he saw that she was dressed for the day.

Gillian had her bright face on. Apparently she was choosing to act as though nothing had happened. "Checking out the local haunts?"

"And the townsfolk," he drawled wryly.

She didn't look at him. "Anything we can use?"

He shook his head. "Not yet. You want some breakfast?"

"Just coffee." She stuffed those seemingly innocent pajamas into her bag. "But if you're hungry—"

"Nah. Coffee's fine. We can get it to go."

"You read my mind," she replied, still too brightly. "I'd really like to get started interviewing Holly Brewster's family and friends."

Checking out at the office, they collected coffee to take along. Settled into the car, he inserted the key in the ignition. Before he could turn it, Gillian put a restraining hand on his.

"Brad, I don't want you to think this changes things between us." She glanced down. "What ended our marriage…well, that hasn't changed, either. We have to work on the case, but—"

"That's all," he finished for her, knowing he was tight-lipped, not caring.

"Don't be mad. I just thought we—"

"I think we've thought enough. Let's get going." He started the car, accelerating so that the engine noise would drown out the need for conversation.

They drove without speaking for several minutes, leaving the town behind and passing rolling acres of farmland and woods. She thought nothing had changed. He wished she was privy to his heart. Then she might not be so sure.

Her voice broke the uncomfortable silence. "Apparently this vic didn't live in a conventional neighborhood."

If she could focus on the case, he could, too. "Not unless there's a new community built out here."

There wasn't. Houses were scattered far
apart, each appearing to sit on at least several acres of land. Brad watched mailboxes
for the number the deputy had given him.
He slowed down. On one the name Brewster
was mostly scratched out, replaced by
Wright. "I think this is it."

After Brad parked on the gravel shoulder
of the road, they both studied the house. It
wasn't run-down, but it wasn't especially inviting, either. The yard was nondescript,
lacking the color of flowers. The house was
covered in green siding, making it blend into
the landscape.

As they got out of the car, a large dog
barked in warning.

Brad glanced at Gillian. It would be difficult to sneak past a dog of that size with a
volume to match.

It didn't seem to matter. No one was
roused by the dog's fussing. They had to
knock twice before the door creaked open.
The middle-aged woman eyed them warily.
"Yes?"

"Mrs. Brewster?" Gillian asked.

"It's Wright now," the woman replied, still looking suspicious.

Gillian showed her badge. "We're here about your daughter."

"Holly?" For a moment the woman looked hopeful, but the light in her eyes faded when a man called her name from inside the house.

"Is Mr. Wright home?" Brad questioned. She nodded.

"May we come in?" Gillian asked in a tone that suggested there wasn't an option.

Reluctantly, Marion Wright pushed the screen door open and stepped aside.

Brad caught Gillian's gaze. Most parents would be anxious to speak to someone who might be able to help them locate a missing child.

"Who're they?" Floyd Wright asked belligerently when he spotted them.

"FBI," Gillian replied calmly. "Mr. Wright?"

"Yeah. This about the girl?"

The girl. Now, that was a warm term. Brad checked his immediate anger.

"It's about Holly," Gillian replied, turning to Mrs. Wright. "We have a few questions."

"We done told the deputy what we know," Mr. Wright answered for his wife.

"We don't always ask the same questions," Brad told him. "Humor us."

Floyd Wright didn't look amused. He lit a cigarette, blowing the smoke in their direction.

Gillian consulted the file. "I understand that you last saw Holly about six o'clock on the evening of the seventeenth. Yet you didn't report her disappearance until noon on the eighteenth. Where did you think your daughter was that night?"

Mr. Wright snorted. "Doing what she always did."

"And what was that?"

"Staying out all night with trash."

Mrs. Wright's eyes watered briefly, but she didn't rebuke her husband.

Gillian briefly met Brad's gaze. "Mrs. Wright, do you have any reason to suspect Holly might have run away?"

Mrs. Wright looked at her husband, then down at her hands.

"Girl was pregnant," Mr. Wright told them with what seemed to be a degree of satisfaction.

Gillian glanced between the Wrights. "Are you certain?"

"No," Mrs. Wright said, finally speaking for herself. "But she was dating this one boy a lot. I was worried—"

"All my wife ever done was worry about that girl. Good riddance, is what I say."

Mrs. Wright slipped a crumpled handkerchief from her pocket and wiped at her eyes. Clearly she didn't share her husband's opinion.

"The boy's name?" Brad asked.

"Luther Freeman," Mrs. Wright replied.

Gillian asked a few more questions, collected the most current picture of Holly and concluded the interview.

"I've never seen a better case for running away," Brad told her as they drove down the road.

"That poor woman."

"She doesn't have to stay with him," Brad replied, having wondered the entire time why Mrs. Wright did.

"Some women don't consider that an option."

But Gillian had. She'd walked away quickly, bloodlessly.

But there wasn't time to dwell on that. Or his resentment that she wanted to forget last night.

Quickly they drove to the next addresses in the file. Interviews with Luther Freeman and Holly's friends cemented their opinion that this girl had run away. Although they had been reluctant to admit it initially, the girls confessed that Holly had confided her wish to leave home and Callville forever. They weren't certain she was pregnant. But she was definitely unhappy. Luther was less forthcoming about the pregnancy, but confirmed that Holly had spoken frequently about leaving home.

Since she was under eighteen, Gillian called the bureau, requesting that Holly Brewster be put in their national search bank.

"Nothing about this girl fits with the other two," Gillian mused. "Rural versus suburban, tight neighborhood versus isolated farm country, the ages. And the case in Tyler wasn't identical to Tamara's or Katie's."

"Thinking they aren't connected?"

"I'd like to check in with the task force, see if they've run down any more disappearances on the carnival's route."

Brad put the car in drive. "Yeah. I'd hate to be wasting time that might make the difference for Katie and Tamara."

Gillian nodded her agreement, then flipped open her phone.

Learning that the team hadn't made any more connections with the carnival, Brad agreed with Gillian that they should return to Houston.

The car ate up the miles. Still, the time seemed to drag since they hadn't been able to dissolve the strain between them.

"Penny for your thoughts," Gillian said finally.

"They're pretty grim."

"I can take it."

But Brad wasn't as certain he could verbalize them. "I was just thinking about how scared those kids must be."

"They're so young to be away from their parents, everything they know."

"And I'm wondering if Tamara's still alive," Brad admitted. "Or even Katie."

"Yeah." The one word sat heavily between them.

In the quiet that followed, Brad thought about something else that had been bothering him.

Gillian seemed to sense his worry. "What is it, Brad?"

"Thinking about the pregnancy thing with this teenager."

"Oh?"

Brad glanced at her, wondering if he should continue. A strange note had entered her tone. "Do you want to talk about this?"

"Sure."

"If she was pregnant, do you think Holly should have told her boyfriend?"

"Yes." Gillian's voice was still strained. "Parenthood is too important not to be discussed thoroughly."

So it was. "Gillian…" But he couldn't find any other words, not any that didn't sound lame.

The previous tension seemed mild in comparison to the charged atmosphere in the close vehicle.

And they weren't even halfway to Houston.

WHEN THEY WERE FINALLY back in the city, Gillian's cell phone interrupted the terse silence just a few miles from the station. It was her partner, and Savino's news wasn't good. As Savino talked, she urged Brad to drive faster. Briefly telling Brad what was going on, she parted with him at the precinct house.

Hell had more than broken loose. Their investigation was splashed all over the media. Although the local news outlets had reported Tamara Holland's and Katie Johnson's disappearances, they had now somehow learned of the two other cases. Speculation that there was a serial killer on the loose in Texas filled the televisions, newspapers and radio broadcasts. Parents were bringing their children inside and locking the doors. A fearful, expectant mood seized the city.

The fact that the publicity had exploded was yet another thorn between Gillian and Brad. When she phoned to tell him the extent of the damage, he thought she'd overridden his concerns and released the details to the press. She hadn't.

Combined with the tense end to the morning, Gillian didn't think she could handle much more personal turmoil in addition to the case.

After speaking with Shawn and Debra, Gillian felt sure neither had leaked the story. The other two possibilities were Vicki Campbell and Roger Turner.

Gillian didn't think Vicki would do anything that might compromise the investigation.

That left Roger Turner. Gillian suspected he would love to be at the center of a high-profile case. He hadn't liked being shunted off to do the same work as the other detectives on the team. She also guessed Roger had thought he'd be the one appointed to head the task force.

But she didn't have any evidence that he was involved with the leak.

It was equally possible that a member of the press corps had overheard a discussion or intercepted a cell transmission. Either way, they were now up against a rapidly diminishing deadline.

CHAPTER TWELVE

LATE THAT EVENING, Gillian reached Brad's apartment in record time. Despite the pressing severity of the developments in the case, Gillian's thoughts had strayed to Brad again and again.

Considering the events of the previous evening and their tense day, she only wanted to escape. She couldn't blow the case by remaining with Brad. Her bags were still in his apartment, and she wanted to retrieve them. The menace of an unknown intruder paled next to the prospect of reliving her past one moment longer. And if she spent another night in Brad's arms, she would be too tempted to forget how monumental their differences were.

He'd left the door unlocked. Once inside she greeted him, then headed to the bedroom, emerging with her bags. "Thanks for the hospitality, Brad. I'm very grateful."

He frowned. "What are you doing?"

"Going home."

"But that's not safe."

"I'm sure our perp's too occupied by the media assault to worry about me."

"Gillian, you're not being logical."

She increased the grip on her bag. "Brad, I need to go home."

"Then I'll go with you."

Gillian shook her head, not trusting herself to spend another night with him. "If I run into any trouble, I'll call you."

Brad opened his mouth, but she cut him off. "You can argue the rest of the evening, but you're not going to change my mind."

His lips thinned, and she felt pangs of regret. Knowing she couldn't give in to them, she left his apartment and drove toward home. Alone in the car, she gave in to the weariness plaguing her.

Despite the fatigue and strain, she realized she missed Brad. Stopped at a red light, she passed one hand over her forehead. How could she have been so stupid? She should have known that spending so much time with Brad would reopen not only wounds, but the feelings she still had for him.

And making love with him…that had been the monumental folly.

Once home, she parked in her space, a bit reluctant to go in now that she'd arrived. She thought of the warmth of her parents' home or Teri's. Despite her assurances to Brad, she couldn't risk leading the perp to her family. She loved them too much to put them in danger.

Opening the car door, she walked to the rear of the Eclipse to get her bags from the trunk.

"Hello," Brad said quietly, standing on the other side of the car.

Startled, she stared at him for a moment. "What—"

"Let's check out your apartment. Then, if you insist, I'll leave you alone."

She guessed that meant he'd stake out the apartment from outside. Not knowing what to do with Brad, yet glad to see him, Gillian nodded. "Okay."

One eyebrow inched upward at her acquiescence. "Why don't we go inside before we get the bags out of the trunk?"

It sounded as though he'd already made up his mind that her apartment would be unsafe. But Gillian didn't argue the point.

Entering the apartment, everything appeared normal. Gillian turned to Brad to make that announcement and saw his face change. Following his gaze, her stomach dropped. The video camera she'd had installed in the living room mantel clock was gone. The tiny camera had blended very well in the piece, its disguise nearly perfect. She was chilled to think that someone had studied her apartment so well they'd been able to find the camera.

She and Brad pulled their guns at nearly the same instant. He motioned with his head toward the bedroom. Hugging the wall, they entered cautiously. But the room was empty. The video camera directed toward the French doors in the bedroom was gone, as well.

Gillian swallowed the lump in her throat. The break-in itself didn't unnerve her, but the violation did. What had the perp touched? Examined?

Immediately she thought of Tamara Holland and Katie Johnson—innocent, helpless. "He's devious…cold…" She couldn't voice the enormity of her reaction.

Brad angled his face toward her. "Gilly, we have to run this latest info through the bureau's computers."

"I was thinking that, too. Maybe we'll hit a match."

"We have to keep this guy off the scent," he mused aloud. "Because he's obviously enjoying the hunt. We can take your car back to the precinct lot, get a cab, then pick up my car once we're sure no one's following us."

Gillian swallowed. She knew what Brad left unsaid. He didn't want to lead the perp back to his apartment. Then they wouldn't have a safe house. "Okay."

The ride to the precinct and then back to her apartment was remarkably quiet, broken only by Brad's terse instructions to the cab driver. They took a circuitous route that would be difficult to follow.

Once back at the apartment they climbed into Brad's SUV, where he'd stowed Gillian's bags. She was surprised when he didn't head back toward his place.

"Are we being followed?" She discreetly pulled down the visor to glance in the mirror.

"I don't see anyone." Brad turned again, the fourth time in as many blocks. "But the guy who broke into the apartment was good. He may have an equal talent in tailing cars." Opening his cell phone, he punched in a telephone number. He asked his father to drive to a nearby mechanic's lot, briefly explaining why he needed to borrow one of their cars. He also asked that his father take a cab home before they arrived.

"Won't that endanger them?" Gillian asked as soon as he'd completed the call. "I can get another car from the bureau."

"Which the perp could spot in a second. I'm making sure that no one's following us." Brad headed down a long stretch of road. "Of course this street's flat—we *are* in Houston. But what is rare is the lack of traffic. It dead-ends into an airplane hangar that we can park behind. If anyone's following us, we'll know."

Gillian stared at the unfamiliar road. "I don't see a street sign."

"Private road. That's what makes it ideal. People don't drive this street unless they're going to the hangar or they're lost."

Gillian was very glad he was on her side. They made it to the end of the road with no one in sight behind them. Brad sped up in the last quarter mile, finally driving behind the huge metal building with a screech of tires. Getting out, they waited at the edge of the hangar's side, out of sight but able to see far down the road. After fifteen minutes it was clear that no one had followed them.

Still Brad was careful as they drove back up the road. With no side streets or places for a car to hide, they were able to see that the road remained empty. Yet Brad continued his evasive maneuvers.

Gillian was still worried about putting Brad's parents in harm's way. However, she had to admit his plan was good. He had phoned the mechanic, explaining that he would leave the car for a tune-up.

When they reached the lot, Brad quickly pushed his keys through the night drop-off slot while Gillian hid in the back seat of his father's car. Just as rapidly, Brad donned the jacket and golfing cap he'd asked Thomas to leave in the front seat. They sailed out of the lot scarcely a minute after they'd arrived.

A few miles later, Brad turned to speak over his shoulder. "No one's following us."

Cautiously Gillian sat up, glancing out the rear window. "Looks that way." She exhaled before the realization struck her. This was only the beginning of a night spent with Brad.

LATE THAT NIGHT the cell phone rang incessantly. Sleepy and disoriented, Gillian pushed aside the blanket as she reached for the phone.

Her drowsiness faded as she listened. Glancing up, she saw Brad at the doorway, equally alert.

She reached for the notepad on the end table, scribbled on it briefly, then clicked off the phone. Staring at the words, she slowly pulled the sheet of paper from the pad.

"Gillian?"

"They found her body." Gillian cleared her throat. "Tamara Holland. She was in the backyard of an abandoned house."

Brad crossed the room, yanking open a dresser drawer, retrieving a pair of jeans. "Who responded to the call?"

"Uniforms." Collecting herself, Gillian reached for the shirt and slacks she'd worn that day. Conscious of Brad's presence, she stepped into the walk-in closet to dress.

Accustomed to the need for expediency, both were ready and out the door in minutes. Although Houston's streets were never empty, there was little traffic to slow them down at one in the morning.

Flashing emergency lights lit up the street that had been cordoned off, and members of the CSU combed the area. Vans parked haphazardly around the scene announced that the press had arrived.

Gillian turned to Brad. "I'm meeting Savino. You can't be here."

Although she could see it cost him, Brad nodded. "I'll park behind the Channel Eleven van."

"I can catch a ride to the station."

She reached for the door handle, but he snagged her arm. "I know you can, Gillian, but I'll be here just in case."

Swallowing, she nodded, then ran from the car.

Just in case.

THE DARKNESS OF THE NIGHT had lifted, but the morning was gray and threatening. Gillian had ceased tasting the bitter coffee she consumed.

But she couldn't erase the taste of defeat and rage she'd felt at seeing Tamara Holland's body. Captain Maroney and her boss, Edward Phillips, had gone in person to notify the girl's parents.

A new edge of desperation gripped everyone involved in the case. Katie Johnson might have only hours or minutes left.

Gillian called the task force together. They studied the storyboard assembled in the squad room, reviewing the facts. Although she briefly cautioned them about releasing any more information, she didn't probe into the source of the leak. There simply wasn't time.

Having no leads was disastrous. Having thousands were nearly as bad. Gillian scanned the pages and pages of reported sightings that had come in to the station within the past twelve hours. Even with four other detectives and nearly a squad of uniformed officers it would take days to sort through the leads. It was almost fatally easy to discard the obvious crank calls. But what if the obvious was also the truth? If they ignored the wrong tip, a child could die.

While the team tackled their assignments, Gillian decided to work on a hunch she had. It was time to put her idea into the federal computer.

BRAD CLICKED OFF HIS cell phone, pondering the change in his parents. Even though they were concerned after the bizarre car exchange, they were in control. Not ready to fall to pieces as they once would have done.

Brad was grateful, but also somewhat disconcerted. He had shared the special bond of loss with them for as long as he could remember. Now it seemed they were ready to move on. He knew it didn't make sense, but he felt as though he were being left behind.

That, combined with the night he'd spent watching the investigation from arm's length, had him rethinking the way he handled himself. Maybe Gillian was right. Maybe it was time for him to move on, as well.

The discovery of Tamara Johnson forcibly reminded him how long it had been since Katie Johnson had vanished. Seventy-four percent of children murdered by non-family members were killed within the first three hours of their abduction. Could young Katie continue to defy the odds when Tamara apparently hadn't? He hoped the coroner would be able to establish the time of Tamara's death quickly.

Gillian's most recent call had let him know that volunteers continued to search woods and fields, but Katie's body hadn't been discovered.

Of course with the new publicity, people were tracking all over the area, primarily getting in the way. Now dogs trained to scent out human remains had also been brought in.

Brad wondered if they should widen the search, taking it in another direction. Interviews in the girls' neighborhoods had gotten them nowhere. Maybe it was time to move beyond the self-imposed boundaries.

Spotting Gillian's car, he waited impatiently, wanting to discuss his thoughts. She stepped from the car, her face wary.

In the privacy of his own vehicle, Brad sighed. Lord, they had a mess of baggage to deal with.

She slid into his SUV. "I don't have much time. I left Savino in charge, but the station's still under siege from the press and public."

"Any forensic evidence from the scene?"

Gillian shook her head. "It wasn't the murder site. She'd been dumped there."

"And from the body?"

"The heat, humidity..." She stared ahead, as though willing away the image. "Nothing yet."

"Is there a preliminary estimate on the time of death?"

"It's hard to pinpoint. Six to eight weeks."

Tamara Holland had been missing eight and a half weeks. Which meant the perp hadn't kept her alive more than a week or so. That was bad news for Katie. She'd been missing for less than a week, and in these cases, the time between crimes usually lessened.

"Gillian, have you thought about taking the investigation in another direction?"

"Such as?"

He outlined his thoughts. "I'd like to widen our parameters, check anything child-related. I'm thinking amusement parks, specialty shops, anywhere our perp could have encountered the victim."

"You mean he may have specifically targeted these girls? Watched them for a while?"

"We've been trying to put together a profile of the perp based strictly on what we know about Tamara's and Katie's abductions. But what if we factor in the way he's zeroed in on you as a threat?"

She nodded slowly. "The bureau profiler

has the information. I can ask him for another analysis.''

Brad realized his own participation might
end with the disclosure. But he couldn't consider that. Instead he thought of Katie and
prayed she was still alive.

''Where do you want to start?'' Gillian
asked, flipping open her phone.

''Panda Park. It's not far.''

''I think I've heard of it—rides and car-
toon characters,'' Gillian mused.

''That's the one.'' Brad wove through the
growing stream of traffic. As he drove, Gillian called Savino and the profiler, then up-
dated her boss. From the end of the conversation he could hear, Brad guessed Edward
Phillips wasn't overjoyed with her report.

Gillian glanced at Brad once she concluded the conversation. ''Don't ask.''

''Then can I ask something else?''

''Sure.''

''Did the profiler see a link between the
case in Tyler and ours?''

''Other than the carnival, no. Vicki and
Shawn haven't learned anything that can

connect any carnival employees to the crime.''

Brad spotted the Panda Park sign and turned in. ''Did they check on casual laborers the carnival hired locally?''

''Carnival owners aren't the best record keepers. But they would notice if they hired the same people in Tyler and Houston. The profiler has the information on both other girls. He doesn't see the older girl fitting at all with the younger ones.''

''Ironic, isn't it? The Wrights, at least Mr. Wright, didn't want their daughter back. And it's all the other parents can think of.''

Gillian's eyes flashed with understanding. ''Like you were with Amanda.''

Not that Brad wanted the Wrights' daughter to be harmed. It was just difficult understanding fate. ''Yeah.''

Brad parked the SUV close to the entrance of the kiddie park. There wasn't a formal office, just a counter with a cashier who directed them to a woman standing amid rows of picnic tables.

Hearing the nature of their mission, the woman was immediately sympathetic. ''I'm not sure I can help you. I didn't know any of those girls.''

Brad met Gillian's glance. Already the public had lumped them together. ''We're doing fact-finding right now. Do you have large crowds during the week?''

The woman shook her head. ''Not really. We sell individual ride tickets and that brings in a few people.'' She gestured toward the balloons she was attaching to overhead rafters. ''But most of our business comes from birthday parties. Usually they're held on the weekends, but we get the occasional one during the week. We furnish hot dogs, the cake and party favors. Parents find it a lot easier than trying to entertain children at home.''

Brad's mind clicked as he heard her words. *Children's parties, keeping them entertained.* ''Thank you. You've been very helpful.''

The woman looked puzzled. ''Well, I'm glad, but I don't see how.''

''I'm with her,'' Gillian told him as they reached the car. ''How did that help?''

"We haven't found Katie's body, despite massive searching that's still going on."

"Which gives me the hope that she's still alive."

"Exactly. What reason would the perp have for doing that?"

Gillian's face grew grim. "A multitude of horrendous options."

"And in the remote chance it's not torture, how would he entertain a young girl?"

"Toys, dolls…"

Brad drove out of the parking lot. "Or a party."

"That's a far stretch."

"True," he admitted. "But what if we check out all the toy stores and party shops?"

"We can run a computer analysis and narrow down the areas that have both in close proximity. I can divide the grid between the team."

"Thanks, Gillian. I know it's only a hunch—"

"Sometimes we have to follow them."

As head of the investigation, Gillian could

have quashed his idea. And his instinct was strongly urging him to pursue it.

Not only for their young victim's sake, but also for Gillian's. He was terrified that her time was running out, as well.

CHAPTER THIRTEEN

THE CASHIER IN THE PARTY goods store
pursed her lips, contemplating Brad's question. "Well, there was this one guy. He was
real picky about what he was buying. He
wanted everything imaginable for a party,
but the weird thing was he only wanted two
of each item. I asked him if he was sure he
didn't want more. Who has a party with only
one guest? But he said that was the perfect
party. Didn't make any sense."

"Do you remember how he paid?" Brad
asked.

"Cash. I commented that the bills were
brand new." The clerk frowned. "He didn't
seem to like that."

"Can you describe him to a sketch artist?" Gillian asked.

"I think so."

Gillian pulled out her phone. "I'll have

an officer pick you up and drive you to the station.''

Stepping outside onto the sidewalk, Gillian glanced up at Brad. ''Good instincts.''

''If it pans out.'' He pointed across the street to a bank. ''And if our perp is confining himself to the neighborhood, he might use that bank to get his crisp new bills.''

Gillian frowned. ''Why so close to the scene? He has to know the entire city is being searched.''

''Why choose exposing himself by stalking the FBI agent on the case? It's part of the thrill, the control, the power.''

Gillian ignored the shiver his words caused. ''We can have Fulton and Turner get the bank security tapes and go over them.''

Her phone rang. Listening to Vicki, Gillian felt an affirmation that they were on the right track. The cashier in a toy store nearby had remembered a man purchasing two identical dolls. He'd stood out in the cashier's memory because when asked if the dolls were for his daughters, he'd clammed up, paid, then left without waiting for his change. The cashier was already en route to the precinct to meet with a sketch artist. Gillian instructed Vicki to coordinate that sketch with the one made by the clerk from the party store.

Brad lit up at the news. "Maybe this is it. And just maybe we'll be able to save this girl."

Gillian felt her throat tighten, wondering how different her life might have been if Amanda had been found. Glancing at Brad, she realized how desperately he needed this case to be solved successfully.

Together they decided to check out a few more places before doubling back to pick up the sketches. The candy store they entered seemed a likely place, but the clerk didn't remember anyone out of the ordinary.

As they turned to leave, Gillian noticed a little girl on her own. Despite all the publicity, apparently her parents weren't keeping her locked safely away. As she watched, a man entered the store and still the little girl wandered unsupervised.

Brad completed his questions and turned to leave, but Gillian stayed him by snagging his arm. "Let's wait for a minute."

Brad followed her gaze, lowering his voice. "Is something wrong?"

She shook her head, her focus on the child. The man took another step closer. Instinctively, Gillian did as well. When he reached the counter, she tensed. But just as she was about to stalk forward, the little girl turned away from the glass display case and the man remained, studying the rows of candy. At about the same time, the girl's mother appeared from the back of the store and took her hand. They headed outside together.

As Gillian stared after them, she wondered how parents ever drew a safe breath. Children were so vulnerable, so fragile. In less than a minute they could be snatched away, gone forever. Gillian nearly choked at the realization. This was how Brad had always felt. That to bear a child could also mean losing a child.

She felt the blood drain from her face.

Brad gripped her elbow. "Come on, let's get out of here."

On the sidewalk, she took big gulps of air.

"What was that all about?" he asked,

leading her to a concrete bench that circled one of the tall, leafy trees.

Swallowing, she wasn't sure she could tell him. Briefly she closed her eyes, thinking of the pain that unspoken words had already cost them. "I think I finally understand how you feel."

When she hesitated, he took her hand. "Go on."

"Your fear of losing a child. Logically I've always understood. But emotionally I'm not sure I ever fully grasped how paralyzing that is."

"What brought this on? The little girl in the candy store?"

"I thought the man who came in was going to try to take her away. And I realized just how easy that would be. On a professional basis, I've always known that. I guess since we seem to be getting closer, seeing another little girl..."

Brad gently increased the pressure on her hand. "Don't be so hard on yourself. It's difficult to understand a loss like that unless you've experienced one."

Gillian kept her head downcast, the irony

of his words refusing to be still. It was time, she realized, to tell him the truth. "Brad, that's not true. I did have a loss. A significant loss."

He said nothing, so she looked up to see a dumbfounded expression on his face.

She continued. "When I was in college, I became pregnant. I went into premature labor late in my fifth month." She felt the hot whisper of tears as they slid down her cheeks at the remembered agony. "The baby was so tiny…. He only lived a few hours."

Brad's voice was hoarse. "Why didn't you ever tell me?"

She wiped at her tears. "I didn't want you to agree to have a baby out of pity."

"Oh, Gilly." His arms pulled her close. "I can't believe you kept this inside so long."

The tears refused to stop. And although Gillian doubted the wisdom of burying her face in his shoulder and allowing them to flow, she let herself sink into his comfort. She cried not only for the loss of her baby but of their love, their marriage.

She pulled back finally, her eyes scratchy,

her throat raw. Sniffling, she reached to wipe her eyes, but Brad checked the motion.

Ever so gently he eased his thumb over the tears. "I'm so sorry."

She took a shaky breath. "You didn't even know me then."

"I'm sorry I made it impossible for you to tell me when we were married. Gilly, I'd do anything to change that."

She searched his face, then accepted his embrace, fitting her head against his shoulder in a way that was not only familiar, but right. And the smallest seed of hope blossomed.

TERI WIPED THE KITCHEN counter, erasing the final evidence of a long day with three energetic children. Thank goodness they were all napping, even though that rarely lasted long enough to get the family room completely tidy.

Four-year-old Dallas wandered through the doorway at that moment, rubbing at his eyes.

She didn't mind that he was awake. Although she wouldn't admit it to her equally harried friends, Teri missed the little monkeys when they weren't underfoot. She scooped him up and began tickling his neck with light kisses. He giggled and kicked chubby legs.

"Should we go see if Kevin and Rachel are ready to get up?" she asked, carrying him toward the bedrooms.

Kevin, the other twin, still slept blissfully. Pulling up his small quilt, she decided to let him sleep a bit longer. Quietly humming a tune for Dallas's benefit, they strolled into Rachel's room.

Teri scrunched her eyebrows together when she saw that the bed was empty. "Rachel?"

No one answered.

"Is Rachel hiding from us?" she asked Dallas in a conspiratorial tone.

With an indulgent smile, she walked to the louvered closet. "Hmm, I wonder where she could be." She opened the door, but the closet was empty except for clothes.

Teri looked more carefully around the room, setting Dallas down so she could see properly. Rachel wasn't in her room. Once awake, she usually played with her dolls, collecting them for their "snack." But the dolls remained on the window seat.

Assuming Rachel was in the bathroom, Teri checked there next, but still didn't find her daughter. Frowning she headed down the hallway. Perhaps Rachel had scampered into the family room, hoping to surprise her mother. When she wasn't there, Teri's concern became real. Despite her young age, Rachel was a creature of habit. What on earth could have made her vary her routine?

Telling herself not to overreact, Teri quickly looked throughout the house, but couldn't find Rachel. She dashed into the backyard. *Surely, Rachel was out there. She had to be!*

But she wasn't. Fear came cold and fast. Teri searched the side and front yards as well. Stomach roiling, she called the neighbors on each side and across the street, then her husband and Gillian, all the time praying. *Dear God, don't let anything happen to her!*

"WE'VE PHONED THE NEIGHBORS we know," David told Brad. "And they've each taken a street. Teri and I have called all her friends.'' His face was grim, determined. ''I'm going to find Rachel if I have to rip open every door in Houston.''

Brad knew exactly how the other man felt. He laid a hand on David's shoulder. ''We won't stop until we find her.''

Police filled every room in the house. Uniformed officers, detectives and bureau agents all crowded the once peacefully cozy home.

The crime-scene unit was busy, trying to find any clue to help. Suzanne and Frank Kramer had arrived, as well. Suzanne had taken over the care of young Dallas and Kevin, freeing Teri. The other Kramer siblings were arriving now, too, wanting to be involved in the search.

The responding patrol officers felt the intruder must have found an easy way into the house. Teri insisted that all the doors and windows had been locked. The intense heat and humidity in Houston made it impractical to leave windows open, and Teri's house was cool from central air-conditioning.

Brad immediately connected the break-in method to the one used in Gillian's apartment. In and out, leaving no trace.

Search and Rescue had been notified and they had joined the local police and sheriff's department already looking for Rachel. Copies of the composite from the sketch artist had been distributed. Volunteers were nailing that, along with Rachel's picture, to anything upright in the area.

Gillian had clung to her sister when they arrived, offering her support, but Brad had seen the agony on Gillian's face. He knew her well enough to realize she felt at fault.

The Kramer family strength was evident as Teri and David insisted on searching themselves. There were plenty of people to man the house and neither of them wanted to sit by and let others look for their child. Gillian assigned an agent to go with them.

Then she approached Brad, her face haunted.

He pulled her toward a relatively quiet spot. "Gillian, don't do this to yourself."

Slowly she shook her head. "But—"

"But nothing. You couldn't have expected the perp to connect you to Teri."

"He must have begun watching me the first day I was assigned to the case."

"He's smart," Brad reminded her. "But he's not smart enough to evade all of us. Do you want to stay here or canvass the blocks around the party and toy store?"

She looked undecided, then a determination he recognized filled her face. "They have enough searchers here. I'll go with you. Our only real hope is to find his hiding place. I'd like to believe that Rachel will be found playing in someone's yard, but I can't take the chance that won't happen."

Brad didn't care if the entire HPD and FBI surrounded them, he pulled Gillian close. She resisted for a moment, then sagged against him.

"We'll find him, Gilly. And Rachel will be all right."

THEY HAD SPOKEN TO EVERY shopkeeper for blocks and no one recognized the man in the sketch. But neither Brad nor Gillian was ready to give up. They stood at the last corner of the grid they'd canvassed.

Brad spotted a small grocery store to the north. "The guy has to eat."

Gillian scanned the streets in the other directions. "Okay."

The store was a throwback to past times. While slightly larger than a minimart, it lacked the size and inventory of modern grocers. This was clearly a neighborhood shop that catered to a small, familiar clientele. One freezer contained all the frozen food, and a single display showcased all the canned goods. It wasn't a store that could compete in any fashion other than convenience and familiarity.

A middle-aged man stood behind the sole checkout counter. "Can I help you?"

Gillian and Brad showed him their badges and then the sketch.

"Do you recognize this man?" Gillian asked tensely.

The man raised his eyebrows at her tone, then took the sketch. "Looks like the guy who lives with Mrs. Carstairs."

Brad tensed as well. "Has he been in lately?"

"Yeah. Mrs. Carstairs usually does most

of the shopping, but he said she wasn't feeling too good.''

''When was this?''

The man scratched his head. ''Tuesday. Funny thing, she was in the day before. I remember because she had really crisp, new bills. The ones the guy had the next day were the same.''

''Do you have his address?'' Gillian questioned urgently.

''In a manner of speaking. I have Mrs. Carstairs's address. She runs an account near the end of the month when her social security money is low.'' He pulled out a worn cardboard file box, digging through the dog-eared cards. ''He ought to be in a good mood when you find him.''

''Why is that?'' Brad asked.

''He bought cake, ice cream and punch. Looked like he was getting ready for a party.''

Gillian and Brad looked at each other. The man handed them the card. The address was only a few blocks away.

''Time to call in reinforcements,'' Gillian

said, punching in the bureau's number on her phone.

"And I'll call Maroney to get HPD backup." Brad pulled out his own phone.

Her eyes searched his as the phone rang.

"I can't worry about my career right now," he told her.

As soon as backup was summoned, they raced to the car and drove the scant distance to the house. Parking across the street, Brad and Gillian split up to question the neighbors. They couldn't be sure they had the right man. But if they did, they didn't want to tip him off, possibly prompting a gun battle that could endanger the children.

It took only a few minutes to learn that Mrs. Carstairs hadn't been seen in a week and that the neighbors hadn't been allowed inside to check on her. Her boarder insisted he was caring for the older woman and that she couldn't be disturbed. The neighbors assumed he had taken off work to do so since his van remained in the driveway.

Van. The choice of abductors.

Gillian and Brad ran toward Mrs. Carstairs's home. The weatherbeaten house had two stories and a wide porch with sagging steps.

Steps that would creak in warning.

Brad motioned with his head toward the windows. Covered with curtains and a layer of grime, they revealed nothing.

"Mrs. Carstairs is older," Gillian whispered. "She'd probably rent out the top floor so she wouldn't have to climb the stairs."

They both looked upward. There weren't any room air conditioners in sight. Nor was there a central-air unit on the ground. But no windows were open at the front or sides of the house.

Staying against the exterior wall, they moved to the back of the house. Two windows were propped open.

"I can't see anything," Gillian whispered. "Can you?"

"Nope." Brad studied the layout.

"Do you think we've got the right guy?"

"My gut says yes. What about you?"

She nodded. "It all fits."

Just then a weak but distinguishable cry floated from the window. "Mommy."

"Front door," Brad spit out as they pulled their weapons.

"Side," she said.

As they sprinted to the two entrances, police and FBI cars, sans sirens, sped onto the street.

Gillian pulled at the side door but it didn't budge. Solid wood, it wasn't penetrable. Running to the front, she saw that Brad had broken the glass at the top of the curtained front door, reaching in to unlock it.

He turned, meeting her eyes. "You take the downstairs."

She knew he was trying to protect her. Still. She followed him into the darkened house. Although sunshine lit the day, not much of it penetrated the musty interior.

The living room was empty, as was the kitchen. Gillian looked down a long hall with two doors. Both were closed. She yanked open the first one, finding an empty bathroom. Taking a deep breath, she opened the second. An old woman sat in a rocker, her arms and legs bound, her mouth taped. Seeing the woman's thin chest rising, Gillian knew she was alive.

Dashing back down the hall, she saw agents, detectives and officers running up the walk. "Cover the side door," she ordered one officer. Gesturing to a second officer, she pointed toward the bedroom. "And take care of the woman in there."

She reached the staircase. "Spiers, Campbell, with me." The rest followed as she ran up the stairs. Three doors stood open. Motioning with her head, she directed the agents to two of the doors. She and Spiers approached the third. But they froze at the doorway of the bizarrely decorated room. Streamers and balloons were strung everywhere. A small table was set with paper plates, cups, elaborate party favors and a cake.

Brad and the perp were squared off, guns aimed. The man's features were unremarkable. Thin blond hair and sallow skin were equally forgettable. Combined with a soft body and rounded shoulders, he didn't look very threatening.

Brad's gun was steady, pointed at the man's heart. The perp's gun wavered between Katie Johnson and Rachel.

Spiers spotted Brad. His sudden surprise switched immediately to confidence.

"It's no longer one on one," Brad told the perp calmly. "Your odds have gone down. You want to risk it?"

The perp's gun jerked upward as he looked toward the doorway. Brad's gun fired at the same instant. The perp looked first at Brad in disbelief, then at the blood that ran down his chest before he staggered and fell.

Gillian stepped into the room as young Katie Johnson flung herself against Brad.

"It's all right," he told her gently, holstering his gun, then picking her up. "You're safe now." He removed the now-grotesque party hat while patting her back.

Rachel ran to Gillian. Holding her niece tight, Gillian felt her throat work with emotion. Not only was Rachel safe, but Brad had finally been able to reverse the tide. He had rescued the girls, changed the outcome, and she could see from his face that it moved him beyond any words.

Biting her lip, Gillian tucked Rachel's head against her shoulder. And watched the man she loved.

CHAPTER FOURTEEN

BOTH GIRLS WERE TERRIFIED but unharmed. Nine-year-old Katie Johnson had refused to be parted from Brad, calling him the hero he had proved to be. He had taken her home while Gillian returned Rachel to her sister and brother-in-law. Holding her child tight, Teri had wept in gratitude. Then she and David absolved Gillian of the guilt she felt by connecting them to the case.

Mrs. Carstairs was weak and frightened. Hospitalized for observation because of her age, she had an excellent prognosis. Her weak sight and hearing had kept her oblivious to her tenant's activities. Unable to climb the stairs to the second floor, she hadn't been a threat. But he had snapped after taking Rachel. A stray comment from Mrs. Carstairs had frightened him into tying her up. She was still shocked by her tenant,

Vance Smith's, actions, having believed him to be such a nice man.

The bureau was running a check on Smith. So far, they hadn't turned up much. It was as though the man hadn't existed prior to this crime. Knowing he had to be a blip on someone's radar, they were digging deeper. The gunshot wound to his chest had been fatal, but before he'd died he'd bragged that he could snatch a child faster than parents could blink. Although weak, he'd seemed determined to gloat about his stalking of Gillian. They'd also recovered her stolen video surveillance cameras in the room where Smith had held the girls.

Sadly they hadn't learned anything about the ten-year-old in Tyler who had disappeared. But seventeen-year-old Holly Brewster had been located in a Dallas shelter where she was safe, enrolled in job training. After notifying Holly's mother, Gillian had spoken with the girl, urging her to call home.

Teri and David were still clutching their children closer, and the entire Kramer family continued to celebrate young Rachel's return. Although the experience had been harrowing, her family's outpouring of love would heal any emotional wounds.

Gillian had arranged a meeting with her boss to explain Brad's role in the case. But first she wanted to speak with Captain Maroney. Even though she valued her own job, Gillian felt compelled to clear Brad.

Maroney wasn't easy to read. Although the man lacked any obvious signs of anger, Gillian guessed they were there. After all, he'd ordered Brad off the case.

She considered a number of ways to approach him, then tossed caution out of the window. "Captain Maroney, I doubt you know this, but I'm Brad's ex-wife."

Despite Maroney's seasoned professional aura, surprise covered his long, thin face.

But she didn't allow him any time to reflect. "And I know him better than anyone else."

Maroney regained his taciturn expression. "Then you know I ordered him to stay off this case."

"Yes," she answered truthfully, not caring what damage it caused her. Earnestly she leaned forward. "I also know that it isn't in Brad to ignore the disappearance of a young girl." Briefly she told him about Amanda. "Now you know about his sister. And you know Brad. Could you expect any less of him?"

The captain watched her carefully. "You're awfully protective for an ex-wife."

She acknowledged. "Maybe. But you couldn't find a better cop than Brad."

Maroney picked up his coffee, had a leisurely sip. "I know that."

"Then—"

"He has a future here." The captain took another drink of his coffee. "Question is, does he have one with you?"

"A HUNCH?" BRAD ASKED HER a few hours later.

"I put together the facts of Tamara's and Katie's disappearances and analyzed similar crimes. It helped to add in the party paraphernalia since another crime scene contained the same materials. Probably one of the very few times he slipped up. It's premature, but I believe there's a slowly progressing pattern that's stretched out over the past sixteen years. In fact, it began around the time Amanda vanished.''

''You're not saying you think this is the same guy who kidnapped Amanda?''

''I can't honestly say one way or another. But when the computer came up with a grid of the crimes, it's a nearly perfect circle that extends outward from Houston, then retreats in the same way.''

''Like a bull's-eye?'' Brad asked in disbelief.

''It seems that way. One of the most marked similarities is the lack of physical evidence. The perp or perps were excruciatingly careful, like Vance Smith. I think when he deviated to follow me he couldn't cope with the changes that caused, which made him uncharacteristically careless. That or he believed after all those years that he was invincible.''

''Makes sense. Any other similarities in the cases?''

''Only two of the bodies have ever been found. Then there's the time span between crime sprees. There are exactly three years between each one.''

''That would be quite a coincidence.''

''That's what I thought.'' Gillian hesitated. ''Did you ever try to link Amanda's disappearance to any unclaimed Jane Does?''

''Of course. But we never came up with anything.''

Gillian prayed she wasn't stirring false hope. ''Do you know if Amanda was ever fingerprinted?''

''I don't think so. We didn't have any reason to believe her prints were on record.''

''If her elementary school participated in a safety program, they may have her prints on file.''

''I'm willing to try, but we've checked out every possible lead over the years.''

''In Texas?'' she questioned quietly.

''Of course.'' Then it struck him. ''You think he may have gone beyond the borders?''

''One of the matching crimes on the national computer bank was in Louisiana. It's not a stretch to believe he could have dumped the bodies outside the state the crime occurred in.''

"To find Amanda after all these years...." He met her eyes. "Even if it means there's no chance she's alive."

"We have the technology to match the prints from a younger child to someone older," Gillian told him, knowing it was probably a futile chance, also knowing they had to pursue even a minuscule lead. She gripped his hand. "I didn't tell you about the pattern before because I didn't want to build up your hopes. There's only a slim chance. Remember that."

He returned the pressure. "I'll take what I can get."

IT TOOK ONLY TWO DAYS to link the prints Amanda's school provided with a Jane Doe discovered in Louisiana a few months after Amanda's disappearance. At the time of her abduction, the information from state to state wasn't connected by a national data bank as it was now.

Brad used his connections in the department to get the body exhumed swiftly and returned to Houston. Until the confirmation, a tiny part of him had wanted to believe they would find Amanda, older, perhaps unaware of her real family, but miraculously all right.

Instead, he helped plan his sister's funeral.

He expected the day to be bleak. Instead it was a perfect day. Although bright, the sun wasn't sweltering and a light breeze cooled the air. The gathering was small since they had decided on a private graveside memorial.

His parents were sad but restrained. So many years had passed since they'd held their daughter, had fully believed in her safe return. Still, tears escaped as the minister spoke and they remembered the lively, beautiful girl Amanda had been. She would have liked the day, he realized in surprise. The gentle song of birds and the chatter of squirrels as they chased up and down the giant, towering oaks. And the thought was a good one.

Brad felt Gillian's hand in his, silently

offering her support. And that was good, as well.

The minister completed the service with a prayer for the Mitchells. The flowers, roses and daisies, were Amanda's favorites and they added a poignant sweetness.

Gillian placed her other hand on his mother's arm. "I'm so sorry."

Elizabeth looked at her with newly regained spirit. "Don't be. We needed this closure. All of us. Gillian, life has no guarantees, and I know now we should make everything we can of each day we're allotted. I regret the many wasted years. But I'm not going to dwell on the past any longer. It's time to face tomorrow."

Gillian hugged her former mother-in-law.

"You will come to the house, won't you?" Thomas asked her. "It will be a small gathering."

"Of course."

"I'll drive her," Brad told his father.

He watched his parents walk away arm in arm, realizing, despite their sadness, it was the first time they'd had a future in many years.

As he drove toward their home, Brad pulled off the main road.

Gillian straightened, looking out the window. "Where are we going?"

"Don't tell me you've forgotten this place."

She turned to look at him. And it was obvious they were both remembering the same thing. It was a spot they'd used for romantic picnics. A special, poignant, meaningful place.

He parked the car and turned off the engine, the silence sudden. But Brad knew he had to brave the many silences between them. "Will you walk with me?"

She turned toward him, her eyes searching, her voice subdued. "Yes."

As they walked beneath the thick canopy of overhanging branches, Brad realized Gillian had never looked more beautiful. The black of her dress didn't detract from her appearance, instead the dramatic color enhanced her translucent ivory skin and dark, flowing hair.

He took her hand. It felt so right within his. Everything in his life was better with her beside him. They paused on a lush, grassy slope and he faced her. "I've been thinking about what my mother said. Do you really believe life has no guarantees?"

She lifted liquid eyes. "Yes. And even though it's difficult, life comes with loss as well as joy."

Loss he now knew they both shared. "Gillian, would you consider changing your job?"

Visible exasperation gripped her. "Haven't you learned anything from all we've been through?"

"I don't mean completely give up your job. But I thought you'd want to be a full-time mother. I know some bureau employees work part-time from home, in less dangerous positions, ones that allow them enough time for their families."

"Oh…"

Brad knew he was tackling the riskiest but most important mission in his life. "I love you, Gilly. I never stopped loving you. And even though it's taken me awhile, I believe our lives would be fuller with children." He swallowed. "What do you say?"

Her lips trembled, and tears she couldn't suppress flooded her eyes. This was what she'd dreamed of, longed for. But even though she loved him desperately, she couldn't ignore the past. "You have to *want* a child. Just as it couldn't be an impulse generated by pity, it can't be a compromise."

"It's not. You asked me if I'd learned anything. I have. I've learned I have to be willing to love...and to lose. I've already done both with you." He stroked her cheek. "And I'm willing to risk loss if it means having children with you, ones I can love with all my heart."

She bit her lip to stop the trembling.

Brad drew her closer. "More important, I know I never want to be without your love again. It's the one constant that's never wavered, only grown."

Her arms crept around his neck. "I've never stopped loving you, either. I never wanted to. I always hoped—"

His lips fitted against hers, echoing the hope that had been etched in their love.

They swayed together beneath an ancient

oak, pledging eternity. The breeze whispered around them, carrying away the pain of the past while August roses released fragrant promises in the sunshine. Promises Brad and Gillian were always meant to share.

*   *   *   *   *

For information and tips on safeguarding our children, download the "Personal Safety for Children: A Guide for Parents" publication from the National Center for Missing and Exploited Children at www.missingkids.org; or the Polly Klaas Foundation Child Safety Kit at www.pollyklaas.org; or call 1-800-THE-LOST.

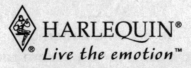

HARLEQUIN *Super*ROMANCE®

3 Women   2 Kids   1 Cat...
All together Under One Roof

Get to know Jo, Kathleen and Helen, three strangers sharing a house. Circumstances mean they won't be strangers for long. At the same time, you'll meet Ryan, Logan and Scott—the three men who are about to change their lives.

It's the family you make that counts.

Under One Roof—
a new trilogy
by Janice Kay Johnson
starting in July 2003.

Taking a Chance (Harlequin Superromance #1140, July 2003)
The Perfect Mom (Harlequin Superromance #1153, September 2003)
The New Man (Harlequin Superromance #1166, November 2003)

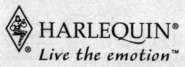

HARLEQUIN®
Live the emotion™

Visit us at www.eHarlequin.com

HSRUOR

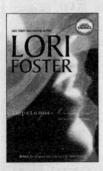

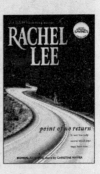
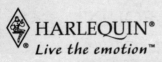

BETTY NEELS

Harlequin Romance® is proud to present this delightful story by Betty Neels. This wonderful novel is the climax of a unique career that saw Betty Neels become an international bestselling author, loved by millions of readers around the world.

A GOOD WIFE
(#3758)

Ivo van Doelen knew what he wanted—he simply needed to allow Serena Lightfoot time to come to the same conclusion. Now all he had to do was persuade Serena to accept his convenient proposal of marriage without her realizing he was already in love with her!

Don't miss this wonderful novel— brought to you by Harlequin Romance®!

HARLEQUIN®
Live the emotion™

Visit us at www.eHarlequin.com

HRBNAGWS

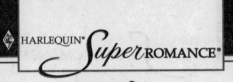

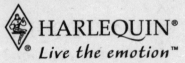